WHO WILL WIN THE BLOODY CASTELLAMMARESE GANGLAND WAR?

It is 1929 and the underworld bosses are choosing sides.

Will "Lucky" Luciano, fugitive of a mob-style vendetta, go with Joe-the-Boss Masseria or the old-world Castellammarese? What about Lucky's lifetime pals, trigger-happy Bugsy Siegel who can't resist a pretty face, and money-genius Michael Lasker whose beautiful wife despises his crime-riddled career?

"Stick with your friends," is mobster Arnold Rothstein's advice.

But who can tell friend from foe, kin from killer, when the Mob revolution begins and America's crime network is blasted apart.

THE GANGSTER CHRONICLES

IT WAS HOT THEN—IT'S EVEN HOTTER NOW...

THE GANGSTER CHRONICLES

BY
MICHAEL LASKER AND
RICHARD ALAN SIMMONS

A JOVE BOOK

First Jove edition published February 1981

10 9 8 7 6 5 4 3 2 1

Printed in the United States of America

Jove books are published by Jove Publications, Inc.,
200 Madison Avenue, New York, NY 10016

To:

Alice Goode-Elman who assisted me in the telling of my story in more ways than one.

M. L.

Preface

The author of these memoirs, who calls himself Michael Lasker, was never one of my own acquaintances. His manuscript came into my possession through a maiden aunt, a former show girl with whom he had many times been on terms of the greatest intimacy. "Nephew," she said, "if you call yourself a writer and don't fancy Michael's memoirs, maybe you ought to consider becoming a CPA."

Upon leafing through the many pages thereafter, my initial skepticism was further compounded by the writer's overly taciturn and phlegmatic turns of mind. If these were indeed the memoirs of Mr. Big, I thought, a name synonymous with organized crime in America and abroad, what he had to recollect initially seemed squalid, at best, and, at worst, horrifying.

Lasker envisioned all the fabled big hitters of legend as essentially greedy slobs—moronic and crude. He did not glamorize his occupation; killing, he constantly, irreverently argued, was just a hard sweaty dollar. I thought who would want to see the great Dutch Schultz reduced thusly?

Then a second more leisurely reading, at my aunt's indecent urging, convinced me otherwise. Lasker and all his associates may have had grievous faults of character, but I thought all would agree they had lived out one hell of a story. That he is still around to tell it to us in person is a miracle on the order of Odysseus' return from Troy or Jimmy Hoffa's disappearance.

Lasker today is a thin, frail, aesthetic-looking fellow

with leathery skin and simple tastes. His poor health, as he points out, keeps him largely housebound. He writes in a small clerkish handwriting on large sheets of yellow-lined notepaper, and also dictates. He claims nothing more than what is due him, and little less.

As all should know, this fellow has only briefly served time for his offenses against the social order. To this day he is considered by some, a few at least, to be an upright citizen of the republic. So this is, perforce, a work of more than mere literary interest: like Motley's *History of the Dutch Republic*, or Nick Schenk's *I Was There*, much of our recently lived history is encapsulated here; Lasker was truly a child of his time. He knew many of the movers and shakers of our modern era, and he was instrumental in the formation of modern corporate criminality, the so-called Syndicate, as he here refers to it.

Moreover, through his long association with the late Charles "Lucky" Luciano and Ben (a.k.a. Bugsy) Siegel, Lasker became a permanent fixture in the sunken living room of the American soul.

De Tocqueville says somewhere, "Someday there will be Americans with crooked hearts, and they will all consider themselves either Democrats, or Republicans." How apt that is to what we know now from these memoirs composed on a deathbed.

In editing them for publication from a somewhat longer version, I have let Lasker's conscience be my guide; all that he said remains said, and I have done only the slightest altering of punctuation and correction of spelling. I want to thank my Aunt Annette for first bringing them to my attention: *Ars Gratia Artis*, as we say in Hollywood. The words here set down truly are Lasker's, a celebration of a modern man's infinite capacity for cunning, cruelty, and greed.

RICHARD ELMAN
Tegucigalpa
Honduras

The soul of the sluggard desireth, and hath
      nothing;
But the soul of the diligent shall be abundantly
      gratified.

                                            Proverbs 13:4

Poverty and shame shall be to him that refuseth
      instruction.

                                            Proverbs 13:18

PART ONE

Chapter 1

So help me, I always much preferred making a dollar to a killing. I was just an ordinary business person with ordinary scruples. You know the type: a dollar earned is a dollar saved. Don't go where you're not wanted. Better him than me, etcetera etcetera. As for dying from so-called natural causes, you could keep them, too. If I didn't have to someday soon, believe me you, I just never would.

On my mother's grave I swear it: live and let live, I've always said, unless you're forced to do otherwise; and if you can't make an honest dollar, by all means do it the other way around. As Rabbi Hillel asked so very long ago, "If I'm not for myself, who will be?"

Still and all I never really liked any of the rough stuff too much, though sometimes we had no choices.

The bottom line today is I'm probably worth as much as U.S. Steel and the Worthington Pump Company combined; real estate in Florida and Atlantic City, chicle plantations in Honduras, a very large piece of the action in Vegas, fast food chains, loan shops, cable TV stations, a cheese factory, a Cadillac dealership, a vitamin factory, a number of trucking and fishing fleets, computer chips, potato chips, policy slips, container ships. Anything you could move fast, for a profit. You name it. I've had my hand in making this country the way it is today. For sure! Not to mention all my former convertible debentures, puts, calls, and second mortgages.

3

In Italy I went into partnership with the Bank of the Holy Spirit to produce birth-control pills; and I've had interests at one time or another in Antwerp, Nicaragua, Brazil, Benghazi, Pretoria, Hamtramck, Michigan, and Singapore.

While I accumulated much, I never spent that much. Until recently I took a lot more in than I ever gave back: uranium mines and magnesium nodules from the bottom of the sea were my latest. One of my companies sold high explosive "silencers" to the CIA; still another built all the so-called comfort stations in all the national parks between Maine and Alaska. I've made grand hotels full of waterbeds and blue movies on cassettes, opened muffler shops from Maine to Chicago, miniature golf ranges, schools of motel management, a manatee ranch off Cozumel, and a mink farm in Stone Martin, Ontario.

Nevertheless after all these years being Mr. Big, when they told yours truly it was the Big C swelling his *kishkes* three times life size, I felt just like little Michael in a pickle all over again: helpless. If you know what I mean.

Right away I sold out everything it took me so many years to put together, even some things at a loss, just liquidated the whole works, and put it all into precious stones: gem-cut diamonds, emeralds, Linde star sapphires. The *emmes*. . . .

Two big satchels full became my equalizers. I figured even if I couldn't buy my way out of dying, I could still give the world of high finance a cash-flow problem such as they would never forget me for.

All the people from the Big Corporations begged and pleaded with me; the dollar's dying, it's a dead duck, Michael. If you take all the diamonds, we'll be stuck with just cash. I told them all that was their problem, and so on and so forth, pss, pss, pss.

Such are the ways of the world. A Rockefeller always wants to look good, no matter what he does, but dying like this, I could settle for being a diamond in the rough, because a diamond, even more than God Himself, really is forever.

4

So I became this throwback, this wandering Jew, a hardening in the arteries of modern multinational corporate capitalism. Afterward it occurred to me there'd never be another one like me, and I felt much better. My dying was the world's great loss, not mine.

I really think it's a goddamned shame God is letting me die like this, such a goddamn waste.

When I was younger, I could understand, but not when I got so much wisdom from all these years of living.

A lot worse people than me will still be around after I'm gone. What a goddamn shame, a waste.

I'm supposed to believe in a Creator who wants to junk just about the best thing he ever made?

I tell you, it's like everything else these days: no respect for anybody.

I don't say it's easy having such a brain: a genius on the order of an Einstein in the Syndicate world needs to know he was loved more than once in a little while, but really all I wanted right then and there, after I got the bum news, was to get to Israel before it was all over for me.

To Zion. . . .

Well, the Israelis weren't so hot on letting me come. Even after I started handing out my diamonds like Gelusils, it was no dice. I couldn't even book a reservation at the King David Hotel, much less a tourist visa. Security problems. They're so insecure, goddamned Israelis. Still, as I had certain old business connections, help was on the way, just as soon as my friends knew who to lean on.

Not bad for somebody who was never even bar mitzvah.

My cover story would be how I wanted to endow a school of medicine for cancer research in my memory at Haifa. If it was okeydokey with them, I said they could name it after Momma. So many years dead and so on and so forth.

Finally I was admitted for treatments only, pummeled with X rays, chemotherapy, and enzyme injections. Then they also said, "You're here, so stay awhile. If nothing

5

else, your money is always welcome. No matter what you did to your fellow man, you're still a Jew, and we can use all the money you give us."

So? What did I expect? To be treated like the president of Bamberger's? Or I. E. Du Pont?

They removed my spleen, and I threw in one hundred million dollars in blue whites. I told myself, why not be the big giver for once in your life, Michael? It's better than tax-exempt municipals any day in the week. Do it for Momma's sake.

And what, after all, you're building here in Zion, could be your only living memorial candle, or *yahrzeit* . . .

Afterward I baked myself red as a brick in the Negev, recuperating from the operation, and I took the grape cure in Tiberias. Then I went off to the shores of the Dead Sea to visit a certain Professor Doktor Oscar Erhard Morgenstern for "hydro-salinic therapy."

I didn't get any worse, but I really didn't get any better. As it has been written, the world as it *is* is just as anxiety provoking as the world we actually may know. I was hungry all the time, my cancer thriving all the more.

Despite such exotic treatments my diet remained ordinary, and rather bland, even for a man of my age: for two whole weeks I ate nothing but carp fished from the Sea of Galilee washed down with mineral water. To cut down on all the cigars, the good doktor also made me suck apricot pits.

This really wasn't too bad. A number of other people, also Big C sufferers, were on hand. We played pinochle and gin rummy, and scraped each others' backs for salt.

Professor Morgenstern wanted me to consider "total immersion" in his "biodegradable fundament tanks" to dissolve my tumors as the treatment of last resort. I was pretty close to being a terminal case, he said, so I said what was the point? I never had that much hope to begin with. At age eighty-one my tumors were legion, and I just knew I was a goner. Still I enjoyed all the attention I was getting.

Dying sometimes is just a great big pain in the ass, but

it's not necessarily excruciating. Professor Morgenstern gave me special lemon- and orange-flavored radium pills for sucking, but as he said, with all his European charm, "Michael, eventually I also believe in die and let die. The mud and the baths, they help a little, to keep your mind off the dying, but so does gin rummy or women."

Well, I never believed in anybody very much. Aside from myself.

"How much time?" I asked. "Six months, maybe a year?"

"By Christmas," he told me. "I guarantee it."

"Well," I said, "will I go through it just like this? Or will I become a complete vegetable?"

"You'll become the world's largest Jerusalem artichoke," he told me, "a regular mandrake root, I guarantee it."

What has always set me apart from all the real losers was my pacific nature and a healthy sense of self-preservation. Just like that, by sheer willpower, I went into remission for a while, and the doctors left me alone again.

For some crazy reason, then, in Jerusalem at twilight on my hotel balcony I was remembering the retread business we ran in 1943. A trick of the mind again surely. We had mountains full of retreads in British Honduras and our own freighters to get them here through the Nazi U-boats. You wanted any tires, you came to Michael Lasker and his boys. Generous I always was, to a fault. But business was always definitely business with me.

Once again I now realized just how far I'd come from my squalid origins in Poland: Ellis Island, New York, Florida, Havana, the Vatican. All the people I've known would surely fill up Dante's Inferno.

If you don't learn from history, it's a waste of time.

Reverential with awe for maybe the first time in my life, I told myself in Zion, in that refuge for Jews from everywhere in the world: "If I forget thee, O Jerusalem, may my right hand get broken at the wrist by Sam Giancana or one of his boys . . ."

A self-made man like me gets zapped in his tracks sometimes and then he just has to stop and wonder what it was he had in the first place that set him above all the others. I bet you dollars to doughnuts: I forgot more about business than most people remember.

The long and the short of it was, I came back to the States afterward with a deep suntan and, to be inconspicuous, bought this little condominium in the Century Village; I hired a practical nurse, who looked a lot like Tina Louise, and a male secretary to push my chair, and then I started to dictate into this machine.

Pretty soon there'll be nothing left for me to remember: just dirty dead in a hole somewhere, like Bugsy and the others.

I don't talk to none of my neighbors. Never. I got a Jacuzzi but I hardly ever use it, except for boiling an occasional carp, maybe a yellow tail. All day long I just dictate before I forget—for the sake of a history, of which I am now one of the last living parts; and so that future generations of nice boys and girls in America really will know what it felt like all these years to gain the whole world and not even risk a nickel.

Azoy!

Chapter 2

It's such a long long time ago, 1908, when I came here from Poland. I think Taft was the President. I was maybe six. Who knows? We didn't have any birth certificates. All I can remember is the stink of all the bodies in the waiting room at Ellis Island: sapphires of garlic, dirt, and fear. I didn't have a father. He barely made it out of Poland before he was dead in this country, of overwork. A dray horse for the biggest machine in the world . . .

On Stanton Street on the Lower East Side where I grew up such a long long time ago my playmates were named Romeo Salerno, Gurrah Shapiro, and little Jakey. Later there were certain others: Charlie Lucky, the Sicilian, and Ben Siegel, whom you may have heard called Bugsy.

The Lower East Side in those days was so jammed full of the children of hard-pressed immigrants from all over the world it hurt to walk the streets. We all seemed to live in each other's backyards: dirty alleyways, air shafts, tenements, pushcarts. It looked like hell, just like this big marketplace right in the center of hell, with the buildings all packed tight like lettuce crates.

None of this was ever very cozy or nice. It certainly wasn't anything like what you read about in Professor Irving Howe. Every second person was either a crook, a murderer, or a hooker, or wanted to be, for fun and profit and to break up all the boredom. Just a lot of losers. They all ended up driving taxicabs, I think, or selling clothing off the rack. The Board of Education for life . . . Some of our most colorful local celebrities were called Dopey Benny, Kid Twist, Little Augy, Ma Mandelbaum, Gyp the Blood, and Niggy Roth. For ten bucks you could get a guy's arm broken on almost any corner; it cost twenty-five for the average leg.

The word "smack"—what you call "horse," the stuff?—that's corrupt Yiddish for a taste. When you had the heebiejeebies, pretty soon that's all you ever needed to get you straight again: just a little *"schmeck."*

So it was probably a lot like what people think Harlem is like today, or Bed Stuy. I'm a realist; people are the same everywhere: they stink with corruption and backwardness. So there were just as many pimps as rabbis, and every other disgruntled pimp or taxi driver, or sewing-machine operator was either a commie, a socialist, a bomb thrower, or some other variety of labor racketeer.

9

I can remember before Charlie and Ben and I got together, I hung out with some of the other immigrant kids: the good boys, like Murray, who became a social worker for the Educational Alliance and never even left the neighborhood, and Phil, who manufactured ladies' suits and coats.

So what the hell do you think we used to do to amuse ourselves? For fun and profit, in the wintertime, we collected frozen horse manure off the streets from the delivery vans and sold it to the Italians on Mulberry Bend, for a few pennies, to use in their backyard tomato gardens.

And in the summertime we'd all just cool off in the East River.

A guy like me didn't have to be too smart to figure out pretty soon there were better kinds of recreation elsewhere.

Let me tell you that was a far cry from the Roney Plaza pool in Miami Beach on the Gold Coast.

My poor old ma used to say, "Michael. This is America, the land of opportunity. Go to school. Be a good boy, Michael. Learn right from wrong."

"We're nothin' here, Ma," I told her. "The only way out of this hole is the dollar. That's right from wrong."

Charlie Lucky's dad was a laborer and stevedore, and he used to say, "The American, first he spits in your face and then he says please excuse me."

But he never liked it when Charlie told him, "Why not spit back, Pa?"

"Show a little respect," he used to say. "What do you know? You're just a punk kid? The Stars and Stripes forever, and so on and so forth."

"You're just a punk grown-up, Pop," Charlie used to say, "and a big sucker, too."

That was after we all started making a living together: Benny and me, and Charlie. Maybe I wasn't a killer, but I did what I had to do, just like any other executive. If a job had to be done, knowing how to find the right people was always my responsibility. The buck stopped with me, even though I never had to stop any bullets.

All told, I only spent three months in the can my entire life. I mean, sure I started out as a mechanic, because I was pretty good with my hands, but whoever said it takes less guts to make a phone call than it takes to pull a trigger?

Somebody has to know how to read a balance sheet. The bottom line was, when I was growing up, the really impressive hoodlums on our block sold ether base and broke legs for Owne Madden and his boys. But they never even knew what a purchase money mortgage was, and they died poor.

As for myself, as a thinker I really didn't start coming into my own until I was maybe thirteen or fourteen, when I got together with Ben, whom you call Bugsy, and Charlie Lucky (a.k.a. Luciano). Don't get me wrong. I always liked good books: books about numbers and business management; also Somerset Maugham and Arnold Bennett. But in my spare time I studied Pittman and the Gregg system. I thought first you should try to reason before you do anything else. One good piece of calculation was worth a hundred bullets. I never chased the skirts. Thank God, I never had to. When I was ready, I married a nice Jewish girl, and much preferred working my slide rule, or the adding machine, to fooling around. But I never was a show-off, even when I started making the big bucks: suits right off the rack and never anything more expensive than a Garcia Vega natural—even when we owned a couple of Cuban cigar factories.

They say all men are motivated by sex or money. Well, I always opted for cash.

Chapter 3

Growing up as we all did, we had this saying: fast quarters are always a heck of a lot better than slow dollars.

In fact, that's how we all got together to begin with. It was nickel and dime stuff, robbing corpses.

On the Lower East Side corpses were as common underfoot as burdock leaves to a country boy. Plentiful, I suppose, would be the word you would use.

Well, this one particular night while some Italians on Mulberry Street were holding a festival, certain other Italians from Mulberry Street were having a little bang-up affair of their own down near the Peck Slip.

They were called Lupo "the Wolf" Saietta and Joe Masseria, and you'll probably be hearing a lot about them before I'm finished. They were, so to speak, the catalysts in getting little Charlie Lucky, who everybody in the world got to know later as Lucky Luciano, together with me and Ben Siegel, whom you call Bugsy.

I don't even remember the name of their victim anymore. He came out of the bar, was hailed by the Italian pair, turned about, started to run, and got two pistol shots in the back.

Saietta quickly left the scene because he was expected first thing in the morning at a christening party over in Fort Lee, New Jersey. But Masseria, even in those bygone days, was a regular artisan of death, and he went right over to inspect his handiwork.

Lucky, meantime, who was christened Salvatore Lucanía, was just a kid, maybe ten years old: big dark eyes, and lots of black hair, crouched behind an embankment all the while. He'd seen the whole shooting like he was this prompter at the grand opera somewhere. When Masseria left to take care of other business, little Charlie slowly and cautiously got up and sort of walked bent over on all fours, like a hunter, toward the body.

He went right to the pockets and turned them inside out: a knife, a rosary, a bunch of keys, and bills, maybe twelve of them, mostly singles.

Just then the festival band started playing "Bandera Rosa," an old Garibaldi song, and Charlie gets startled; he glanced up in the thick darkness and realized he was not alone. Benny and me had been stalking the same kill the whole time from behind a building.

Benny was holding a length of lead pipe: he was always precocious, did his first job at age twelve. He had absolutely no fears, that boy. Four years my junior and not a fear in his head. Never . . .

He looked right at Charlie and said, "That's ours." Then he held out his hand. "Come on . . . come on . . . come on . . ." The menace in his voice was getting more and more intense, a hissing snake. "Will ya come on and hand it over?"

That was the first time I ever set eyes on that little Italian kid who was to become our partner, and right away he impressed me when he reached for this stiff's knife.

I think he would have used it on us, too, except I told him, "Hey, what's the fuss anyway? Take it easy . . ."

I thought maybe we could make a deal. "We make a deal. We split. Okay? Divvies? Etcetera etcetera?"

A face not meant for church, or heaven; the little kid gave no sign of understanding.

"Halvsies," I pleaded. And to Ben, "These Eyties, they don't understand nothing, and so on and so forth . . ."

Benny's now flaming angry. "I'll take that knife and shove it right through him, and then he'll understand."

13

"Pssspssss, Ben," I said. "Friendsies, Benny. Let's make friends. Okay? Everybody understands friends . . ."

I snapped my fingers at little Charlie. "*Amici,* you, me, him. We split: *Divida,* you, me, us . . ."

He was still uncertain so I thought we should all become properly introduced. *"Benjamino,"* I said, "Benny . . . Io *Michele,* Michael. *E tu . . . you?"*

Benny had that pipe raised like the Sukkot *lulov* he was about to shake against poor Charlie's skull. Still he held his ground, with the knife pointed at us, full of menace.

Charlie said, *"Ladrones, cabrones . . ."* (thieves, cowards.) I'm sure he would have said worse to us, if we cared to hear him do it, but just then there was no time for insults. We all heard footsteps. Cops, on the run in our direction.

Benny said, *"Cheese . . ."*

I said, "He means cops. You understand. *Capisci?"*

Still the standoff continued with knife and pipe about to duel each other, like creatures out of Krazy Kat, when Charlie Lucky suddenly winces and flings the knife aside, strips half the money from his hand, throws it to the ground like in a crap game, and takes off into the darkness.

Well, we grabbed off the rest and scrammed, too, in the opposite direction, to our own little hiding place on the opposite side of the square.

These two uniformed members of New York's finest then did just what we did. The first said, "Just another dead wop . . ."

He cased the scene and told his buddy to check out the whole area, like where we're hiding.

Then he knelt down in front of the corpse to go through his pockets, also. But we've gotten it all, and he's disappointed. I doubt if Charlie liked hearing the word "wop," because maybe that's why he did what he did next.

One of these cops was heading right at us, and Benny was ready for him with his lead pipe. From the other side of that square Charlie suddenly stood and pointed at the stiff and said in Italian, "There's a dead man there, Officer. The man's dead. . . ."

Then he takes it on the lam right along the embankment and disappears into the darkness, drawing away both cops with him.

The festival band was now playing "Back to Sorrento" when Ben and I thought it was safe enough to get up from behind those packing cases with our stiff legs and go on home.

Chapter 4

When we saw him again Charlie told us that he slid down a drain pipe into a sewer in order to disappear. Some moxie he had, even then. It was well past midnight when we ran into him again on Mulberry Street at the fiesta.

The cops' brass band was marching in place to "Mother Machree" and in the hard light of the arc lamps all the big Italian families were turning their faces greasy with sausages and *zeppoles*, and drinking vino.

Charlie Lucky was at a veal and peppers stand when we came by and he'd just paid for his sandwich with a dollar bill, and was waiting for the vendor to count out the change.

I think he was just a little frightened when he saw us standing there. Such cold dark eyes he had, like the eyes of death, just staring at you.

Confronting him like this was all my idea so, as usual, I did all the talking. "Listen," I said, "a fool and his money are soon parted. Once you've eaten all those veal and peppers, Charlie, maybe you want just to talk?"

I gave his arm a squeeze. Benny, who once bit off this

Greek's ear on Pitt Street, was looking pretty feisty too, so I held him back and said, "Come on over here, Charlie."

No dice.

I reached out to him again and again; he shook himself free of me and strutted toward the moving crowd.

What the hell, might as well, I thought at last, and I reached into my pocket for everything except a singleton dollar and pushed it all toward his face.

"Here. It's yours."

"What's this?" asks Charlie, eyeing me doubtfully.

"I'm giving you back," I say. "You give him too, Ben."

"Why should I?"

"Because I say so, Ben. He helped us, didn't he?"

So Ben produces his share from his pocket for Charlie also.

Then I told him, "It's yours. We're friends. *Amici* . . . friends. This is Ben Siegel and I'm Michael, Michael Lasker."

Charlie nodded and tapped himself on the chest. "I'm Charlie . . . Luciano . . . Charlie Luciano."

"Take," I insisted. "So we'll be friends."

He gazed at me like I was some kind of screwball, and then he looked at the money and smiled a little. "Friends." Then he just turned and disappeared into the crowd. He wouldn't even take a nickel from us.

"You see, Benny?" I said. "You see?" It was as if I was driving home some deep lesson to him which sticks to me to this day. Nobody gets nothing never for nothing. You gotta earn; you gotta trust. The reason why even to this day I don't approve of welfare is people should have to work for what they get, even if it's only running numbers or selling dope.

All of us had regular steady jobs as kids. That's how we learned the value of a dollar. Charlie was errand boy in the Goodman Hat Factory, and I was an apprentice at Mr. Paulus's machine shop, and Ben worked in his dad's clothing store where they pulled the customers in with a hook.

Kids nowadays are so spoiled in ways we were never

allowed to be. There was no TV, no radio. Nothing. The only thing anybody did was work, and eat, go to church, and sleep. What we called recreation, I suppose you would call "petty thievery."

But everybody needs a break from the routine sometime. The only thing I ever got for nothing was beef liver at the butcher shop in the old days, but now you can't even get that.

I never was anybody's fool, and neither was Charlie. When they gave away brains, we got double portions, but Benny's was mixed with a lot of kasha varnishkes.

In the end we all settled for friendship.

One day many years later Charlie Lucky told me just what had happened at Mr. Goodman's Hat Factory only a couple of days after our first meeting. Charlie had run off to Mr. Goodman's to get out of the house.

Goodman was, as usual, glad to see him. He gave him a nickel for a package Charlie'd found outside the door, and he let him play with Sheba the cat in the back room. Mr. Goodman always said Charlie had a good heart. "You're a good son, Charlie Luciano. Tell your parents."

So Charlie was feeling a little better by himself playing with the pussycat and a piece of red ribbon in the dark back room behind the curtains, and Mr. Goodman was up front eating his brisket sandwich when they both hear a clicking sound, as if a jimmy or a ring were being knocked against the glass front door.

Charlie squints through the curtains while Mr. Goodman wipes his hands carefully and goes to the front door. And standing right there, with his face pressed against the glass, is Mr. Death himself, Umberto Valenti, another one of Saietta's boys.

He's wearing a big wide-brimmed fedora, eyes like a Jolly Roger's underneath the shadow of it. So Mr. Goodman knows this can't be no social visit, and he closes the blinds. "I'm closed," he says. "Tomorrow. I'm closed right now."

The tapping gets louder, more insistent. Charlie watches his businessman friend go to the front door. As he unlocks

17

it, Goodman asks, "Now what's so important anyway?"

"A courtesy," says Valenti, pushing himself shoulder first inside. He always had this very mild little voice but an evil eye. They say he used cocaine on himself, and chloroform on some of his victims.

A regular gentleman.

Poor Mr. Goodman was not by nature a suspicious person. He fenced an occasional piece of hot goods, but he was basically honest. Though he didn't know Valenti, he recognized the type: a gunsel. And when Valenti said he'd come from Mr. Saietta, and turned and redrew the blinds, Mr. Goodman said he didn't even know any Saietta.

Astonished, Valenti asked, "You never heard of Lupo? *Lupo the Wolf?*"

Poor Mr. Goodman looked like he was reaching for his digitalis, according to Charlie. He tried to beg off. "I have my work. I'm sorry . . . I . . . "

For the moment Valenti was acting kissy sweet. "Please, Mr. Goodman. It's not for me, but for Mr. Saietta . . . For Don Lupo . . . his respect. Just a little token, a gift. Two dollars a week. The layaway plan."

Charlie said Valenti even had eyes for Goodman's sandwich, and the graduation picture of his daughter, Yetta, from Seward Park High School, but two dollars was more than Goodman wished to spend to propitiate any Wolf, like Lupo.

With trembling hands he pretended to get back to work making a beaver ready for blocking.

"Business is off for me twenty percent since Thanksgiving," Mr. Goodman explained. "I got the water bill to pay and my life insurance, and for the cemetery plot. I told all this to the other man. It's just too much."

"It's three weeks now since you told," says Valenti. "That's too much, and too much much. I could die from all your too-muches, and so could you."

Then Mr. Goodman said, "My wife is sick. Got no money . . . the insurance . . . my daughter . . ."

All just a lot of blah blah to Valenti. He said, "If you

18

got money to eat, you got money for Lupo . . ."

"Maybe next week."

"Sure. Next week."

Abruptly he pushed Mr. Goodman around to face him and said with that mild little whisper. "You try. I help you try."

Then he struck Goodman so he fell behind the worktable. Valenti picked up the red hot iron and bent down low over his victim. Charlie wasn't even looking anymore when he heard Valenti say, "Now I'm going to press your cuffs for you. No tickee no washee. Hee hee hee."

There was a scream like the lady next door gave out when she was having her baby. Even worse, says Charlie, louder, and then Valenti gave Goodman a fierce kick too, for good measure, and there was silence.

The gunsel went to the door but he was distracted by Sheba who had come in from the back room.

For a long long while Valenti must have been staring right at where Charlie was behind that curtain. Then he picked up Sheba, just like any other cat fancier, and stroked her, and set her down on the worktable, and left the premises.

Charlie says he took another minute before coming out into the shop and, when he saw all the blood on the floor, he didn't look closer, just panicked and ran out through the curtains to the back room, unlocked the rear door, and went out into the alleyway. His parents' fire escape was right there and Charlie was pulling himself up hand over hand when he felt somebody grab him by the right ankle.

It was one of the same police officers of that murder the night we all met: Officer Hearn. Charlie recognized him by the way he swung his nightstick, sort of nonchalant.

"Where do you think you're going?" asks Hearn.

He didn't recognize Charlie, but he figured he could nab him for attempted breaking and entering.

Charlie didn't know if Goodman was dead or alive. So he reached for the officer's hand. "Mr. Goodman. Come quick. Mr. Goodman."

Charlie wanted to help his friend and he started to lead Hearn toward the back entrance to Goodman's shop.

A sharp whistle came from the other end of the dark alleyway and they looked, and under a streetlamp stood Valenti, with his brim snapped down over his eyes, beckoning like the pope himself.

Hearn said, "You stay here. *Capeesh?*"

He pushed Charlie against a wall and started down toward Valenti, as lackadaisically as possible, without making it seem like he was dawdling too much.

The lamplight washed over both figures like green ink as the officer and the hatted man conferred; Charlie watched.

Then Valenti patted Hearn on the arm, and left, and the cop glanced down the alley toward the boy, and raised his nightstick like a club. "Go on, get yourself home to bed. Get off the streets, boyo," Hearn said, "before I take you in."

Charlie says when Hearn walked away, he stood there in that alleyway a little while longer, and all he could think was *someday . . . someday . . . sooner or later*.

It wasn't so much revenge he wanted from Hearn, and Saietta, Valenti, and Masseria, as a recognition, of sorts, that the worm could eventually turn.

He knew then who he would surely be someday: Lucky Luciano, a very big man indeed.

Chapter 5

You wouldn't have wanted to see where Charlie lived in those days: a shoe box. We all lived in places like that: cold-water flats with toilets in the hall. Charlie was climbing up the fire escape to get back in bed in the tiny cubicle that was his in his parents' tenement flat.

All he had in his room was a broken-backed chair, a bed made from a cut-down door, and a wooden crate for his personal effects which were anything that couldn't hang from the nails on the wall.

That night his mother came in just as soon as she heard the sound of Charlie's footsteps. In her long gray cotton ticking nightgown she was brushing the light spilling through the doorway into her thick faded hair. Her voice was loving and reproachful, "Your father's boots, Salvatore. Come here. You got time to play with yourself, you got time to do this."

She led him into the kitchen to his old man's boots. They were so thickly crusted he had to run them under the sink before he polished them and shined them up.

Charlie says they were iron-toed, weighed ten pounds each, and it hurt to lift them, him being still so frail. While he labored, his mom ran her fingers through his hair.

"Sonny boy. Be a good boy." She left him there in the kitchen polishing, and as soon as she was gone, he found her old teapot, lifted up the lid, and put all the night's loot in with her household money, and crossed himself, and went on polishing again.

A couple of days later was a shape-up on the docks and Charlie stood there with his old man wearing those spit-shine boots as the contractor called out names: "Urimento . . . Marchi . . . Calvelli . . . DeLucia . . . Santucci . . . the two Santino brothers . . ."

Finally all except the old man Luciano had work for the day, and then the contractor shrugged his shoulders and spread out his hands and smiled a little weakly. "That's all there is, there ain't no more. No more work for anybody."

Poor Mr. Luciano was dumbfounded. "What about me? What's wrong with me?"

The contractor just looked over at Charlie. "Your son has got a big-mouth problem. It's just much too big for your boots. No work today for you, Salvatore, so you'll have the time to teach him a lesson."

I guess that contractor thought the old man would really give his son a licking such as he would never forget, but despite the bitterness he felt as a poor man deprived of a day's pay, maybe more, Charlie says his father's eyes were gentle when he glanced at his son.

He touched the boy's cheek and said, "That's for Mr. Goodman. Okay . . . okay." Then he yelled out, *"Bums!"*

"Okay," he said another time as he kissed his son's cheek. All he wanted was the boy should get to school right away. "Go," he said, "to learn, it shouldn't be a total waste."

Chapter 6

Speaking of school, for all of us that was always a losing proposition. Who wanted to be a full-time CPA? If you couldn't go to Harvard, or Yale, the rest was rotten herring, from P. S. 3 on up.

We went because we had to go is all. Myself I could take it maybe just a little, if the weather wasn't too nice, but Ben played truant from kindergarten on, and Charlie really wasn't much better. All the time bored. Especially when they made him stay after hours in detention.

The teachers all thought he couldn't speak and understand and they treated him just like a dummy. "You're stupid. You'll never learn. Do you *even* know what stupid means? *Stupido!* Is that Eyetalian enough for you? Strunz! You want me to say it to you in Italian? Don't ya even know what country you're in?"

Just imagine: this twenty-dollar-a-week pedagogue talking that way to the future Lucky Luciano.

They kicked him out as many times as they made him stay in detention.

Once he threatened a teacher with a pencil box because she called him a "dumb dago." Charlie may not have known really good English then, but he knew when he was being called names improperly.

That was the last time you ever saw Charlie near a school. When he came out on the street looking as if he were about to kill, there were Ben and me on both sides of him. When he walked faster, we caught up to him. We were all friends now, buddies, partners till death do us part, and as we grew up together, nothing changed between us. Except our looks: Ben, with his fine easy strut and movie-star looks, was always a clotheshorse. So was Charlie, but he was less *shtark* than Ben: slim, and dark, a little guy. I was seventeen, or eighteen, and not so much of a looker. As I've said before, with me the brains always counted first. The way I looked physically, I could have been a watchmaker, or a fine surgeon. I had sensitive features and good hands.

As we grew up together, the girls always went for Charlie and Ben; I got the real woman.

But who had time for that? In our teens we were each taking in forty or fifty a week off this and that, aside from the straight jobs we held to help out our families.

Ben's dad, the clothier, was a regular crook of his own devising. A customer came in for a suit and he'd have Ben stand in the back behind the curtain and he'd show the man a suit and call out to Ben, for the price, as if he were calling out to one of the hired help, a perfect stranger, "Jack, how much for an XK-92?" And Ben he would have to shout back in a funny voice, "The XK-92? That's thirty-one dollars."

"For you I'll make it twenty-one," says the old man.

"Sold," says the customer for a suit worth maybe twelve fifty.

On the side the old man also ran a hand book and a bucket shop for stocks and bonds, but he wasn't very partial to any of Ben's enterprising ways. There'd been some rabbis in the family, including some said—the Gaon of Vilna. Whenever Mr. Siegel asked where his son had been all the previous evening, Ben would tell him he was with Luciano and Lasker talking to some girls.

"Don't give me from girls," said old man Siegel. "Where do you talk? What about? In busted warehouses? With a crowbar?"

Seems he regarded me and Luciano as common hooligans, not fine enough for his Ben. The Siegels had high hopes for their Ben. Probably they wanted him in the suit business, "honest and decent" just like they were. They'd give competition to Witty Brothers. Or with his good looks he should marry a manufacturer's daughter uptown at Temple Emanuel.

Be "honest and decent," and always take good care of number one.

Ben always said, "The only other person as honest and decent as my old man is in Sing Sing doing time for shaking down old widows."

He was some crazy kid, that Ben. Used to sing, "I am too beautiful for one girl alone," and really mean it.

And he really liked skirts from the millions on up.

Me, as I say, it was all with my hands and my brain: a medieval mind at work, a Rembrandt maybe.

You gotta understand that. I never had many problems with my self-image. Ever.

Which is why I never fancied being blamed for what happened to JFK.

I never would have dirtied my hands like that, never would have touched him with a ten-foot pole. He was the President of the whole country, and I was always a patriot.

Even in the old days I was like that: sensitivity to the tips of my fingers, and tactful, too.

Lord God Almighty. . . . Even when my old boss Mr. Paulus would ask me to work overtime, and I knew we were having a crap game at the Butternut Loft on Peshine Avenue in Newark, say, or somewhere downtown, like the Grand Street Boys Club, I always tried to decline in a tactful way. I'd show him this book I had on modern business management and say I had a class to take at Pace Institute or Rand.

He always said, "Go. Try to improve yourself, Michael. It's a land of opportunity." Opportunity for the games started about the time we were sixteen. We moved from place to place, staggered the nights and times. I ran the games; Ben placed the bets.

It was a good living.

25

One night we had a visitor, Hearn, now Sergeant Hearn, prosperous and sleek, like a pregnant seal under all those brass buttons on his blue coat. His face, though, was the same cast granite. He pushed open the doors to the loft where we were and moved toward the action boldly.

Ben looked alarmed, but I warned, "Easy, Ben. Make friends."

Sergeant Hearn recognized us both, and he came over to the players and stared right at me.

"Michael Lasker."

"Sergeant Hearn, as I live and breathe."

"Common gambling," he sputtered. "Common gambling's against the law."

I said, "We're all just friends here, Sergeant. You're welcome to try your luck."

I handed him the dice.

Hearn gave me a cold fishy look. "And break the law myself?"

"Try the hard eight," I said. "Make two fours—ten to one on a dollar."

"I'm a poor man, young Michael," Hearn said. "So how would I have a dollar to be gambling away?"

"So I'll trust you. Do me something," I said.

Hearn did me just like I thought he would. He picked up those dice and rolled them, and as the dice came across the felt at me, I took the cap off Ben's head and covered them just when they stopped rolling.

Only I could see he'd done it the hard way then. "Two fours is a hard eight. Shooter wins ten." We counted out two fives for the sergeant. He took the money, as if collecting evidence. "Game's over for the night, boys."

He started for the door. "Michael Lasker, should your game move elsewhere, you'll be sure to keep me informed."

"Absolutel positivel, Sergeant."

Ben was very peeved with me afterward. "That dumb mick never made it the hard way."

"That's what he made."

"My ass," said one of the other players.

26

Everybody was laughing. But Ben had very little humor. He threw his cap at me. "You keep it. You just bought it."

He turned and darted toward the door.

"Game's over," I said. Too late. How I now wish I'd held Ben back.

Because Ben tracked Hearn into the alleyway where he was standing waiting for us all to depart and then he found another piece of lead pipe and gave Hearn a blow to the head that knocked him silly.

Ben rolled Hearn of every cent he took from us, and then he copped his service revolver too, which marked a whole new phase in our operations for Ben, and Charlie, and me.

On the street the next day I met Charlie and I walked him back to Goodman's Hat Factory with a delivery.

We split a blood orange together, half and half.

Charlie asked how the game went last night, and I explained about my donation to Hearn, since I didn't know anything yet about what Ben had done.

He couldn't believe I'd just give away our ten dollars in profits.

"We only made a dollar?"

"You want to play, you gotta pay," I explained. I offered to give Charlie back his investment.

We were right in front of the factory. Charlie blinked and tore off a bloody orange segment and popped it into his mouth.

"Let it ride," he said.

Mr. Goodman was also prospering. No more fencing for him. He was a substantial manufacturer on the up and up, and my partner Charlie was still only his delivery boy, only what he delivered, he delivered for himself, as a sideline.

"Ya know," I used to tease him, "you got an awful lot of spare cash for a fellow in the hat-delivery business."

"Well, I deliver a lot of hats," he winked back, "and I got this special white powder for preserving the felts."

"White powder, you say?"

"A sort of analgesic," went Charlie.

27

We're standing before one of the smokestacks leading out of one of Mr. Goodman's biggest steaming vats, and every few seconds it belches big white puffballs of smelly rank smoke, like indigestion, and I look and there's Ben sitting down with his new cap pulled over his eyes on the factory steps.

Ben was never very subtle. He asked Charlie, "You hear somebody whacked poor old Sergeant Hearn in the alley last night?"

A Cheshire cat.

Charlie says, "Too bad about the poor sergeant. He ought to complain to his *commendatore, Lupo the Wolf.*" He started to go into the factory, but Ben held him back. "Charlie, I'd never hold out on you. . . . Not you, *or Michael.*"

He reached into his shirt pocket and found some bills and waved them at us. "I got us back our ten."

"You were the guy?" Charlie wasn't exactly incredulous. More like surprised. As was I.

"You, Ben?"

Ben stuffed some bank notes into each of our pockets. "It's ours, isn't it?"

That's the day he got his nickname. Charlie had to go to work, but he was still very angry, and just a little upset.

Depressed is more like it. "You bounce cops in an alley? You're crazy as a bedbug, Benny," he said. "I don't even know ya."

He went inside but I'm left standing there just the same, and Ben is grinning like Teddy Roosevelt's bull moose.

I shoved him against the wall and slammed his forehead like a loving cup gesture, with the heel of my hand. *"Bugs in your head . . . bugsy . . . bugsy . . . bugsy."*

I couldn't stop.

Ben was laughing, and I couldn't help myself. After awhile I was laughing too.

Then I said, *"Bugsy Siegel,* that's you all right," and it stuck, like flypaper.

Chapter 7

As I say, Charlie had a number of incentives for staying on at Mr. Goodman's Hat Factory. He really liked Goodman who was now his oldest friend in America, and he had developed this profitable sideline while delivering hats.

Then there was also Chris, Chris Brennan, who worked there. She and Charlie really had something going for them.

Chris was a beauty, real *shikse* good looks: blond hair, a blowsy sensual air. She always seemed to know she was a knockout, and she clearly had the *heisses* for my friend Charlie.

They had regular signals about where to meet, and when. If she wanted it, even then, she'd just ask Charlie if he had cleaned up Mr. Goodman's basement storeroom lately, and Charlie would ask, "Did Mr. Goodman say he wanted it cleaned up?"

"I just think you should," went Chris, "is all."

Since Mr. Goodman was always looking on in his big office next door to where they worked, the two had to be careful. Still a shape is a shape. Charlie never could take his eyes off her.

One day Mr. Goodman asked Charlie into his office. He was a well set-up middle-aged man nowadays with a suit and vest, and spectacles, and a gold watch fob, but he still wore Valenti's big red badge of a burn scar on his wrist, like a rosette.

Mr. Goodman was an honorable man so he always

29

thought well of Charlie—so well he wanted to promote him, to be a salesman, production, whatever he fancied.

"What do I have this business for?" he would say as if talking to his son. The son he never had.

But Charlie always said he preferred the streets: deliveries.

It just didn't make any sense.

Goodman knew that. He invited Charlie to dinner Friday night. They'd eat, he and Charlie, and Yetta's little sister, Rivka, and the wife, and then play a few hands of pinochle. Just the two of them.

Charlie knew that whenever Goodman won a hand, he got pinched in the nose, so he said, "Someday I'll win. Then it's your nose."

Because they were just like father and son. Closer even than that. He really wanted Charlie in the business, maybe even in his family, but he had to settle for pinochle on Friday nights, and other forms of faithful service.

One day Mr. Goodman cautioned Charlie, "That Chris works for me, she's a *courva*, you know what I mean?"

"What's a curveball?" Charlie asked.

"*Courva*," went Goodman. "It means 'not a nice girl.' A 'whore.' You understand? She'll bring trouble."

Charlie blushed the color of red casket plush. He said, "She ain't anything to me. She's just a girl."

"She's got big ideas," Goodman said. "Bad ideas. *Hot ideas*. You stay away from that type. You want a woman. I'll find you a nice Jewish professional from Second Avenue."

"I don't need that, Mr. Goodman."

"Young men have definite needs," Goodman said. "They also gotta be careful or they can ruin their lives."

"You don't need to worry."

"Don't tell me what I need to do," he said. "I like you, Charlie, and I don't want trouble, for you, for me, for anybody. It's getting better out there. That fat hoodlum, that Joe Masseria, the one who works for Saietta, I hear the police finally got him."

And all Charlie said was, "You still believe in the police, Mr. Goodman?"

In the basement later, on some bolts of cloth, with just a piece of candle for light, Charlie and Chris were naked together. Those two really made such sparks together in the dark it's a wonder the whole damn factory didn't catch on fire.

Afterward they were motionless, and quiet, moribund, as Charlie tried to muster all his defenses: hate, love, contempt, scorn.

"Don't you like me, Charlie?" she would ask.

"It's this place, I guess. I don't like it. It's not very romantic."

"Then take me to a nice hotel someday. You know how."

She pulled him down toward her again and started unbuttoning the shirt he'd just pulled over himself. "But in the meantime, Charlie."

Charlie cupped her beautiful fair face in his swarthy hands, "You know you're crazy. You know that?"

"Because I like you, Charlie?"

"You like everybody. You're a *courva*, Chris."

"What's that?"

"It ain't nice, Chris." He kissed her. Her arms went around him. She pressed her cheek against his, her voice whispering close, "What do you want from me? What do you want to be? What do you want more than anything?"

His lips moved down along her cheek and grazed her shoulders.

"Guess?"

"You want out? You want money? Money's just the same as out. I know what I've got to sell. I bet I could make money at it, and so could you. No more of this nickel and diming life . . ."

Charlie felt hurt, and scared. He had a Sicilian's honor. Didn't want any horns. He pulled away from Chris. "What are you talking about?"

"I know some other girls," she said. "You'd really like them, too. We could all have a place uptown, away from

31

this crummy neighborhood, Charlie."

He told me her eyes glowed like sapphires, her fingertips played with the few hairs on his chest.

"You're strong. You could find the right men, men with money. You'd protect us."

"Luciano the pimp," he snorted. "Charlie the Protector."

He was really so furious there was a rasp to his voice.

"Charlie," she begged. "I'm good. Trust me. It's for you too."

"Thanks for the compliment," he sneered. "You honor my family. Why not try your luck with that slob Masseria?"

He snapped his fingers at her like he'd forgotten. "But oh yeah . . . he was arrested. It just slipped my mind. So try Saietta. You could work one of his cribs."

Chris was also beginning to blaze a little. "You think that's all I'm worth?"

"You want to go peddle yourself," he said, "so have a good time. Whatever I run—whatever I'll ever be—I don't ever deal in women."

But Chris knew him better than he thought she did. A woman sleeps with a man she knows more than just the color of his toothbrush.

"What do you deal in, Charlie? Hats? Is that what you put in those boxes?"

He reached out, as if to hit her, and when she flinched, he softened again, and was tender with her once more, his hand resting gently against her cheek.

He spoke in a whisper, as if his lips were kissing her, caressing.

"I'm not going to hit you. I'm not going to hurt you, Chris. I don't want you to hurt me either. I'm just going to forget what you just said, and you forget, too. You understand?"

While he caressed her face, Charlie reached across for his jacket.

"How much do I owe for the visit?"

Chris smiled, a Lilith, "Charlie, if you had to pay for it, you couldn't even begin to afford it."

He couldn't take his eyes off her again.

"I know what a *courva* is," she said. "So I'm a *courva*. It's a lot more fun than being nice little Rivka Goodman.

"No hard feelings, Charlie." She winked.

He winked back. "No hard feelings, Chris."

But then, maybe to punish himself, he extinguished the candle flame with his fingers, as if in expiation, for something or other; and he had this little burn scar to show for it, until the day he died.

From a little schoolboy's diary Charlie started to write in at the time, which he kept sporadically for all the rest of his life, I see the following set down for that fateful afternoon in the hat factory cellar with Chris B.:

This mark I make on myself is a man's mark, acknowledging the weakness of my flesh. My blood is Christ's blood, too; hammered into his putrifying flesh. The priests say be strong and suffer not Satan. I feel their marks on me sometimes also. When a woman wants me, I want her back, but then I also wish to die, to die and to ascend to heaven on high.

But a man's a man. No doubt about it. I have appetites like any other. I'm no goddamn priest. *O lente lente spiritus nocte* which they tell me is Church Latin for slow slow my soul of night. See how these whores deceive us with their tricks, and fooling around. They are like filth, all women are, and we are so easily deceived by their filthy raiments of flesh, the heat of their caresses. The mother of my children would be different; the soul of Mary in my house. Otherwise I could never surrender to a mere woman. Someday I will be rich and powerful, like Morgan or Root, or I will be the Sicilian Christ, crucified for certain. For nothing less is my life on this earth a passion and a torment. . . .

Chapter 8

In those days life was still pretty much of an ordeal for
Momma and me: a dismal tenement hallway, litter and filth
were our lot, despite the little extras I was making. I couldn't
yet come out into the open. We were supposed to be re-
spectable people. Mom made her living sewing in the apartment for Sterne, a regular Simon Legree.

Eight men and women worked where we lived. They
brought their babies, and their illnesses, and their filth—
sewing women's coats together from cuttings in the dismal
gaslight. They huddled like asthmatic slaves while Sterne,
a cantor's son, lean and desperate, contracted the work for
them for pennies, and plied his own machine in a separate
corner of the kitchen.

Every time I left my bedroom in the morning to wash
up at the hallway sink, Sterne would be there in the kitchen,
sucking on a lump of sugar as he sewed; and the others bent
in their misery over coats and suits, Momma included.

She rented our lousy premises to Sterne for a few extra
pennies, and that way she did not also have to sew herself
blind.

The old Jewish men and women sewed garments with
black thread, like the Fates. They hummed dense lamen-
tations while they worked.

The apple of my mother's eye, I was also the subject of
much interest to Sterne, who called me just Lasker.

Just like that. He wanted to teach me how to sew for

34

him, too. "With a good machine, you always got a good trade."

One day he kept hammering at me to learn how to use one of his machines.

I'd just gotten up.

I was still a little fuzzy in the head. And this long shiny apparition in black was like an accusing finger.

I asked, "Which machine would I get to work, Mr. Sterne?"

He became excited. "Any one. That one, if you like."

He pointed to his own Singer with the automatic bobbins. I wasn't letting him off so easily.

"Is there a sharp needle, Mr. Sterne?"

"Sure it's sharp."

"Well," I said, "change the needle, make it the sharpest you got. Then you know where you can go and stick it."

"Someday you'll beg me," Sterne said. "You'll beg."

But I ignored him and went out the door. When I came back, Ma was up brewing coffee. She had on that Chinese peignoir I bought her uptown at the Stewart's department store, and she was laying out plates of coarse bread and salt herring for the morning meal.

Sterne was hungry. So were the others. He asked Ma to crack open some eggs.

But when she saw me, she looked so pale and ill, suddenly, as she told me to follow her into the bedroom.

It was like entering an opium den. There were swatches of cloth hanging down everywhere, and a damp mildewed smell. But, at least, it was private.

I was glad to see her but sorry she looked so haggard and ill.

"Ma," I said. "I didn't want to wake you."

"I was awake," she said. "Sterne woke me."

"The son of a bitch."

"Don't lose your temper over Sterne," she said. "He isn't worth it. A woman alone in the world like me needs company."

I didn't understand. What was she saying?

"Ma," I said. "Go back to bed. I'll fix you some eggs. I'll make eggs for everybody."

"Sterne too?" she asked.

"What about Sterne?" I asked.

"He doesn't mean any harm. He just doesn't understand. I like him but I love you, my golden son."

"Ma . . . Ma . . ."

I was truly shocked. Disgusted. But I loved my mother. Who was I to judge?

I hugged her and led her back to the bed to sit down.

I would bring her some food. She must eat better, have some fresh air, and sunlight, not this.

"Ma," I said, "someday it's not going to be like this."

"I hope not, my golden son."

"In the meantime," I said, "you and Sterne . . ."

"Your friend Benny was here," she interrupted me. "He brought me some milk."

"A nice boy," she added. I said, "All the pretty girls call Ben a nice boy."

"Well, he's not," she said then.

"Oh yes he is, Mom. He's nice. He brought the milk, didn't he?"

"He's not at all nice," she insisted. "He's not."

"You're just feeling bad," I said. "You drink enough milk, eat enough eggs, you're going to feel a whole lot better. That's a scientific fact," I blurted out. "You know the two best doctors in the whole world? It's a cow and a chicken."

She laughed because she couldn't help herself, and I went into the kitchen to make her some breakfast.

Sterne and his people gave me dirty looks even when I left most of what I had cooked up in the pan for them, and, when I went back into her room, Mom was sitting up in bed propped against some pillows.

"Sterne gave me a baby in my belly, Michael," she said, "but I lost it . . . I was just too old for more babies."

She was getting a little teary again.

"Ma," I said, "someday it's not going to be like this."

"I hope not, my golden son."

I kissed her musty brow and face, wet with her own tears and perspiration.

"In the meantime," I said, "you and Sterne . . ."

"You work so hard," she said, "and then you come home to what? Lust, filth . . . and Sterne. I'm so sorry, Michael."

I loved Ma, but I didn't love her self-pity. She was always the victim, the martyr. I was no victim. Never wanted to be. Still I told her, "It's probably just as well, Ma. Don't fret."

"Sterne," she said, "he means well. I think I'm sorry. Sorry for living, Michael. Sorry for bringing you here to this place."

"What are you sorry about? For missing all those Cossack pogroms in good old Poland?"

"There's a war there, Michael. Maybe they leave the Jews alone now."

"Yeah, well, there's a different war here, right in this room. One of these days you're going to the country, to the Catskills on a farm where you sit on a porch for a few weeks and count the trees. And you eat four times a day, maybe five; and everything's fresh. Eggs big as oranges."

"All this they give away?"

"Nobody *gives* anybody anything, Ma. Not in Poland, not in the United States of America."

"You give to me," she said, running her fingers through my hair. "My beautiful son. My golden son."

"Some beauty."

"Maybe we should never have brought you here."

"No, Ma. America's the best place for a guy like me. The biggest and the best there is, and I'm beginning to know how some of the parts go together. Maybe it killed my father, but it's not going to kill you and it's not going to kill me. And we don't have to be poor. And we won't need Sterne any more. What do you think about that? I'll prove it to you. We'll see when you're sitting in a rocker in the Catskills."

I heard the whirring of the sewing machines in the other

37

room and the kettle whistling and swore that she'd hear birds and trees swaying in the breeze someday soon.

"I'll see," she said. "Someday. Is that a hope or a prayer."

"It's the *emmes*, Mom. I mean it. Someday."

Then I heard Sterne's wheezing wheedling voice, "Mrs. Lasker . . . have you got maybe some tub butter for my herring? Be quick about it, woman. . . ."

Chapter 9

Charlie later told me that on the day his little sideline became a liability, he had come upon Joe Masseria sitting in his car across the street from his parents' tenement. Charlie was the sort who went over to pay his respects without meaning much more than "I got your number."

"Mr. Masseria?"

"Luciano. How's it go with you, okay?"

Charlie was holding a stack of hatboxes in each hand.

"Yeah, fine," he said as if juggling cakes. "I heard you had some trouble—with the police."

"No trouble. The police stick their noses up their own asses. What they going to do to me?"

"Sure. Good luck, *Don M*."

Charlie wanted to take his parents to lunch before he made his final delivery. But on her knees polishing the floor was Mrs. Luciano, her face so troubled he thought there had been a death in the family.

"Sallie, my son."

"Momma, what are you doing down there? You can see your face in it already. Where's my smile? No smile?" He tried to pull her mouth into a smile. "Where's Poppa? Is Poppa here?"

Mr. Luciano walked in with a limp, old and tired before his time, his face somber, a crucifixion.

"You come home for lunch, Sallie?"

"Poppa, my name's Charlie. Sallie's a girl's name. No, I don't come home for lunch. I take you both out to lunch. Come on, we'll go eat scungilli in a restaurant."

"You're so rich all of a sudden?" his father asked flatly.

"Hey, where's the funeral? Somebody die? I want to do something nice, you both got faces down to here."

Charlie didn't suspect a thing, he told me, not even when these two strangers came out of the back room flashing badges.

"Just stand over there, Charlie."

"Who *are* these guys?"

"Over there, Charlie, and spread them." The second guy speaks for the first time when he produces a gun with his badge and displays it.

"Federal agents."

Bent all the way over with his legs spread, Charlie asked, "What are they doing here?"

"They ask about you, Salvatore," his mother told him, the tears forming in her eyes.

"You won't mind if we look at your hats." The first agent smiled as he started removing the bindings from the stacks of boxes and took out the hats.

Charlie's ready alibi was, "They're not my hats, they're Mr. Goodman's hats. All I do is deliver them. What's going on?"

The second agent ran his fingertips over the linings and removed a small packet of white powder after probing under a hatband.

"What else do you deliver?" the first guy asked, tossing the packet onto the table while the second agent checked under more hatbands and removed more packets.

"Salvatore Luciano, you're under arrest for violation of the Harrison Act."

Still on the floor on her knees, Charlie's mother cried and begged, "No please, no . . . *Virgin Mother, please.*"

"Don't Momma." Charlie hated to see his mother in pain, and he hated the humiliation later on of prying fingers looking for more of the stuff. Worse, though, was what happened next.

Mr. Luciano's open hand exploded against his son's face.

"Bum!" Again he struck his son. *"Bum! Liar! No good!"*

Charlie grabbed his father's hand before he was struck a third time and held it away as they glared tensely at each other.

"I'm sorry, Poppa," he forced the old man's hand to his lips, and kissed it. *"Scusi,* Papa . . . *Scusi."*

Charlie's posthumous diaries, which only I have seen, record the day he was arrested as follows:

Momma momma poppa your poor boy Charlie your son . . . forgive him for I knew not what I was doing and I humbly ask your forgiveness so pray for me now as at the hour of my birth. The scandal of it momma . . . never again to our whole family the shame . . . never never never never never never never.

Chapter 10

Poor Charlie. He couldn't have cared less if they had put him in solitary and chained him to the walls. It was the sting produced by his father's hand that hurt him more than anything, a matter of pride and family honor again. That look of disappointment in his old man's eyes broke the poor kid's heart.

As it was, the prison farm where Charlie was sent was something like a summer camp for kids like us from the Lower East Side. Charlie made friends easily. Frank Costello and he became ditch-digging buddies and many of the guards walked around unarmed. For a price they'd get you anything: a man, a woman, a fix.

Charlie's prison diaries, read so many years later, post-humously record the life he led while confined. Day after day the one- or two-sentence entries are like heavy jail doors clanging open and shut on a life of monotony, humiliation, and pain, no matter what one could obtain for pain-killers.

Cruel, hard sentences such as, "Me, I'm nobody's punk, not me ever."

And, "Everywhere here I see man's inhumanity to man, and then what? We all have to sit down later to pork and beans for supper.

Here are some samples from the month of August of the year he was imprisoned. It was the time of the great flu epidemic; even in jail people were dying, like flies stuck to flypaper.

August 1: Hot and sweaty with the grime of boredom. Washed all my underwear...

August 2: Ain't leaving here without a proper education. Learning to don socks from the trustee. I watch a cockroach crawling up the damp stone wall of my cell. What industry. Stick-to-it-tiveness...Regular Henry Ford, or Edison. If all humans were like that we'd be living like millionaires.

August 3: Sundays. Nothing much to do. I had enough church when I was little.

August 4: Some guys are learning a trade here...of sorts. I already know my true trade. Just needs an opportunity.

41

August 5: Frank Costello says you could have fooled him I was Eyetalian until I opened up my mouth. He says any fool can tell an honest to goodness person from a faker. Smart fella, F. C. He'll do well . . . A Jewish girl friend somewhere . . .

August 6: I read in the Confessions of St. Augustine lent to me by Father Albright, the prison chaplain, that he, like me, was at one time pretty wild. Damn near drove his poor mother crazy with worry and fear. Then he became a bishop and found Christ. Maybe Christ is in me, too, as I used to sometimes think: my humble origins like his, too . . . Christ forgive mine enemies but set me free. New York was never the City of God, a devil's swamp . . .

August 7: Hot . . . so hot in here I stink like rotten meat, or fish, and stick my hands up to the wrists in the toilet to cool off a little.

August 8: St. Augustine was a black man but he was unlike any colored we have here. Repentant, whereas here they think the white man's cruelty justifies anything. Me, I will never be a bigot, like some: inefficient. A man's a man is all . . . and I will tell that to the parole board too when the time comes but I will never crawl. I don't even think of girls anymore. Just sometimes that Norwegian broad who ran the bakery . . .

August 9: Boring. What I wouldn't give for a big plate of *pasta al filete de pomodoro* with some of my old man's dago red.

August 10: Honestly, putting grown men and boys together like this must be a torment for the really different ones. In the print shop the one with the hair lip he's a different one, I'm told. No girl would ever have him, cruel world . . .

August 11: Some guys admire atheletes or military men like Foch and Blackjack Pershing. Well I don't. It used to be my heroes were Ford and Andrew Carnegie and the like, but now I admire Italians, Garibaldi, D'Annunzio, leaders of men, with the common touch.

August 12: This place was punishment enough the first day I arrived.

42

I don't miss home but I miss Michael and Ben. My true brothers. Athos, Porthos, and Aramis in the Douglas Fairbanks movie—not these punks.

August 13: I'll never get caught again so help me. This is the last time.

August 23: Haven't been able to write for days. First I was sick and then I almost died, and then the thing I dreaded about being here happened, and it was a thing that happened is all and Frank is sort of angry at me now.

Christ forgive me as I forgive you all your many wounds and your untimely death.

August 26: A death watch over me again. Can't stay put in bed, and hard to stand up, too.

August 28: Christ save me from all those cockroaches and bluebottle flies.

August 29: The hell with God if this is what they call punishment.

August 30: Mr. Jerris the guard looks a lot like Ludendorfer the big German general: a big fat face, chin whiskers, and a walrus moustache. Old-fashioned brute.

August 31: When I leave here I am never coming back. Softball today with FC, TL, others. I knock a homer from a bunt. Sliding into second base another time, after a walk, I have my front tooth knocked loose by 3 F. Later I have to pull it out with a string.

September 1: Harmonica in the next cell playing "Wang Wang Blues." Tonight Bumpus and Wagonstiff both burn.

One day, a few months after that terrible summer, a guard told him, "You got a visitor." Charlie wasn't expecting anybody. Who could care? Charlie figured me and Benny should stay clear of him in prison, but I had my ways of keeping informed as to his condition.

"Me? Luciano? Are you sure?" he asked the guard. "Me?"

"Yeah. Let's go."

"Must be for Frank. I don't get any visitors."

"It doesn't say Costello. It says you," the guard said.

Then Frank told him, "Maybe it's your old man, Charlie, or Chris. I told you to give him a chance."

Charlie was beginning to be fearful again; another slap, another insult in this place could be more than he could even bear. Still he loved his father and hoped he had come in peace. How would he ever know?

"He waited this long," he said, "he can wait a little longer."

"He can, I can't," went the guard. "You coming or not?"

"He's coming." Frank answered for Charlie.

Frank was being Charlie's buddy, not just his punk. By the time Charlie walked the distance across the long dismal field, he was pretty sure it was his old man coming to be his first visitor.

"Poppa?" Charlie said as he opened the door to the visitor's room.

Mr. Goodman sat on the far side of a long table. A prison guard stood behind him.

"Hello, Charlie. I'm sorry I'm not your father. I really am."

"So am I. How is he? Do you ever see him?"

"Fine. He's fine. You hurt him. You know that."

"And Momma?"

"She sends her love and prayers to the Virgin for you. Your Poppa doesn't want her to come here." Mr. Goodman handed Charlie a paper bag. "I brought you some things— toothpaste, candy, soap, just some things. Some corned beef sandwiches, and a rosary from your momma . . ."

"Thank you." Charlie covered up his hurt and put on his tough face again. "Just what I needed, a rosary . . . to pray . . ."

Ignoring him, Goodman said, "You look good."

"Sure. Why not?"

"Drugs, Charlie? How did it get to be drugs?"

"I was delivering the hats. Somebody asked me to deliver something else. That Harrison Act—all of a sudden it's a crime. A couple of years ago they were selling the stuff over the counter."

"You learned a lesson?"

"About the drugs? Yeah. There's laws and laws, Mr. Goodman. Some the police turn their backs to. Drugs—I learned the lesson."

"The police—how did they know?"

"Maybe a girl. I don't know. Maybe Joe Masseria. He was arrested and then he wasn't arrested. Maybe he traded me off. You look surprised. Someday the son of a bitch will pay . . ."

"Listen, sonny boy, I learned a few things in my time. You go for revenge, you better dig two graves: one for your enemy, one for yourself."

Impressed by his old friend's wisdom, Charlie smiled. Goodman had taught him a thing or two, Charlie used to tell me, even if he was a loser.

"They teach you that in the hat business?" he demanded then.

"When you come out, Charlie, you'll come back to me. You'll make a salesman. You count on a job. You'll come to dinner, a little pinochle—you'll get in the nose."

"Thanks for thinking about me. I appreciate it. I got other plans."

"What plans?"

"It's a land of opportunity, Mr. Goodman! That's why my folks came here from Sicily—to pick up all the gold in the streets. I'm not looking to fight anybody; I just want my opportunity. Like the cops and the politicians and the businessmen in their sweatshops. Like everybody else who isn't waiting around for a gold brick to fall on him. Mr. Goodman, I know all about them Rockefellers, and the Morgans, and them others."

"Crooks, Charlie? I eat three meals a day. I make a business. Am I a crook too?"

"You work hard, Mr. Goodman." He took the older man's hand, exposing the fading pink scar. That brand.

"Look what they did to you for all your hard work!"

"You want to be like them? Thugs? Is that what you want? To be a King of the Earth . . . like a Frick or Andrew Carnegie? Or that *goniff* Rockefeller . . ."

"Even better, I'll never be a thug. No disrespect—but I'm not like you either. I got my own scams."

"What sort of scams?"

"Leave it to me," Charlie said. "You? After they burned you that time, did you pay them off—Saietta's people?"

"It was a long time ago, Charlie." Goodman withdrew his hand.

"Do you still pay them?"

"Who's going to protect me? You?"

Charlie thought to himself, *someday maybe*, though all he said was, "You're my oldest friend in America. Tell my mother I love her. Tell Poppa too. Tell him I'll make it right with him. Give me a few years."

"I'll tell them, Charlie. And Charlie, I thought you should know. Yetta . . ."

"How's she?"

"We married her off," Goodman said. "A nice enough young man . . . two weeks ago Sunday at the Central Plaza. He's a law student."

"Mazel tov."

"I wish it had been you," Goodman said. "And that Chris Brennan . . ."

"The *courva*? Is she still around?"

"She went away. A man. They say she went to Chicago. She was trouble, Charlie. You're lucky to be rid of her. *Nafkeh* like that."

"Thanks for coming, Mr. Goodman. Thanks for all the presents." Charlie felt this new wound about Chris like a failure of his own breath. He needed to change the subject.

"By the way, I didn't even ask you how business is?"

"Don't ask." Goodman winked.

"It's that bad?"

"Ippsy-pippsy and couldn't be better," Goodman said. "They say we'll be in the war—in France—any day now. I'll make hats for all the young men. They'll be taking all the young men for corpses, I mean soldiers."

Like Goodman, Charlie was also a pacifist of sorts.

"They won't make *me* a soldier," he said, "because *I'm a criminal*. Ask the police. They wouldn't lie to you."

"Are you so proud of that?" asked Goodman bitterly.

"I'm not ashamed," Charlie said. "Being a criminal these days is almost a sort of privilege."

"Just be careful you don't get yourself killed in somebody else's army," Goodman said.

"Absolutel positivel," went Charlie. "'I don't want a bullet up me arse,' as the great Sir Harry Lauder would put it."

"That's my Charlie," Goodman said. "A realist. He would have made such a great salesman, my Charlie."

But visiting hours were over for the day. Charlie simply said, *"Scusi,"* with his voice thick as he left the room for confinement again.

Chapter 11

The war came and went like all wars—a lot of people got rich, a lot of young men died.

Afterward was a heady time. The living celebrated their good fortune. It was one big party everywhere: lots of money, lot of blondes, and booze, and big fat-cat bellies.

The only problem was with the peace came a new law: Prohibition. Selling liquor anywhere was against the Law of the Land, by an act of Congress, signed, sealed, and delivered by the President of the United States and all those other pious scoundrels.

Just like today, with marijuana. You make a law against what people want really bad enough, and they find a way to get it. Luciano and I didn't invent Prohibition, but we couldn't have asked for anything better. It was our big opportunity. The day they passed that law, the price of liquor doubled, and we celebrated.

I remember the night it happened. Charlie and I were at a club with these two chippies and they had a regular countdown, like the ball dropping on New Year's Eve in Times Square. It was 1921. People were loaded. This place was really posh, a padded sewer with mirrors everywhere you looked, and Charlie and I were dressed up in our best suits, like Witty Brothers' front window. Close like brothers.

The two chippies were pretty enough, as I recall, but nothing special. Dolls without brains; sometimes a man goes for that when he's a little heartbroken, a peroxide dame and a lot of twinkle-twinkle chatter.

But that night was also something special for Charlie and me, watching the johns and their dates cavort with streamers to the noises of champagne corks popping. There seemed to be some kind of unnatural connection being established for us right before our eyes—between what people were not supposed to be doing and what they insisted on doing anyway. A world turned on its head in front of all those mirrors.

Charlie said to me, "Either this whole damn country's going straight to jail, or a whole lot of people are going to get very rich selling what they *oughtn't* to."

"*Shouldn't*, you mean," I corrected him. "Booze is bigger than ever, I think. Bootleg hootch, and what have you. People will drink that girl's peroxide bottles and pay for it, and if you got the real stuff . . . like Arnold Rothstein . . . who has warehouses full of it . . ."

"Arny Rothstein may be a big brain," Charlie said, "but he's certainly not the only one who's got a warehouse, or brains."

I looked at Charlie, as if maybe he was out of his mind.

But he seemed very serious and collected.

Still there was no harm in testing him out a bit. "I'm a businessman now, Charlie. No more jimmying warehouses at two in the morning."

"I'm talking about broad daylight. Legal as a church. With the right partner."

Charlie crossed himself for luck against the evil eye. But I wasn't afraid of any whammy like that. It was the feds who had me worried a bit—the new enforcement people.

Charlie went on, "The law's the law. Who has all the liquor tied up in bond?"

"The law," I said, "the government."

"The government of the United States!" He was getting a little high correcting me. "They made all of this just for you and me, Michael. So I think we better get the law on our side and do just what the government says we should do."

"Are you nuts?" I asked.

Then Charlie's bimbo got restless. "You two going to talk like this all night long, or are you going to talk to us and dance?"

Charlie thought he knew how to handle her. "Listen, beautiful, I think I'm in love with you, because you're so beautiful."

"We only know each other for two days."

"Charlie never falls in love for longer than that," I said. "Go on. Kiss her, Charlie."

He kissed her and said, rasping, "I sure like you a lot, babe."

"What about you, sweetheart?" said my date with her hand on my thigh.

This swell-looking black orchestra played "Bye Bye Blackbird," and "Royal Garden Blues."

We kissed, and drank, drank and kissed, like school kids. Life was long. It was our party. Why worry? Then the hostess came by to ask whether we might care to dine.

"Not at these prices," said Charlie, rising out of his chair.

I got up then too. "Thanks all the same," I said.

Charlie said, "Come on, let's go get some ice cream."

The chippies were a little hungry and disappointed, but they left with us.

At the bar on the way out I thought I saw Chris Brennan with a fat black man three times her age, and if it was her, she would have given Clara Bow a run for her money. I didn't say word one to Charlie who was looking away, distracted, because just then this Texas Guinan–style dish, the hostess, announced, "Come back any time, boys— whenever you've got the cash."

Chapter 12

We really couldn't splurge beyond a certain point because, you see, we were saving all our spare cash for the big job, with a lovely White sixteen cylinder with double wheels. It was my job to make that baby purr like a Rolls, as I'd learned to do from a book. Ben lifted the thing from the Railway Express, but it needed repainting, new serial numbers, and a lot of tuning up and other stuff to be ready for our needs, and that took plenty of our time and money. Ben never quite got the picture. He thought we were just planning another stickup. But when the White was all ready to roll, painted shamrock green, with new plates, armored tailgates, and a gun slot, Charlie finally set him straight.

We weren't busting into any federal warehouse; we were buying our way in; and Charlie, and Ben, and I each would have to put up equal shares of the initial investment out of our savings.

I can still hear Charlie laying it out for me and Ben, like we were a high-school football team somewhere and he was our gipper, Knute Rockne.

"We've got all our money in the world on this table. Every cent we own. We all worked hard for it. We took risks. Now let's grow up—face some facts."

He was speaking mostly for Ben's benefit now. "Nobody, none of us are looking for trouble. Benny, if it comes, I'm going to need you because of your style. Meantime, keep your gun in your pants."

"Gee, Michael and I were all set to shoot the mayor."

Charlie just ignored Ben. "When push comes to shovel, I'm going to take care of the real business and be out there on the point with that fat slob Masseria. Ben'll be with me. I know that's not for you, Michael. You get the rest of it together."

I protested, "I'm not your errand boy, Charlie."

"Whoever said you were?" Charlie was suddenly soothing. "I'm saying you're smart. So you think for us, and I'll take care of us."

"And I'll protect Charlie while he does," Ben put in.

I reached over and pushed all our money into a large single stack.

"I guess this firm's in business."

And Charlie said, "Let's find out," and reached over and scooped up all our money because he had some foundation building to get started.

His diaries record him as resolute afterward:

> It matters not how straight the gate.
> How charged with punishment the scroll,
> I am the master of my fate;
> I am the captain of my soul . . .

Chapter 13

Big Tim Sullivan was Tammany Hall's ambassador to the Lower East Side.

A large florid man with a wide range of gluttonous appetites, he held court during lunch at the Stella Mare restaurant off Mulberry Street most days of the week.

Sullivan wore checked suits and bow ties and always tucked his napkin under his many chins.

The faithful came and touched him, brought him gifts, and asked for favors. One day not too long after our firm was capitalized, Charlie Lucky appeared at this court, like a gentleman courtier from Verona.

Charlie was always a respectful person. He addressed this swollen leprechaun as "Mr. Sullivan."

"Sure and my friends always call me Tim," went Sullivan, extending his hand. "Would you have a seat?"

Charlie was respectful and sat down.

Sullivan poured himself a fresh glass of wine, and asked, "And what would be your name?"

"Charlie Luciano."

"And how can we of Tammany Hall be of assistance to a man named Charlie Luciano with such coal-black eyes?"

"I don't need any assistance."

Sullivan was amused. "Needs no assistance . . . You don't need? You're in good health? Employed, are you? No bones to pick with the governance of this great and sovereign city of New York?"

"No complaints. None whatsoever. As a matter of fact, Mr. Sullivan," Charlie said, "I'd very much like to make a political contribution for the welfare of the party."

Charlie took an envelope from inside his jacket pocket and believe me it was stuffed with greenbacks, as Sullivan very quickly perceived, from a hasty perusal of the contents. He stuffed the envelope inside his pocket, swallowed an oyster on the half shell, and had a suddenly calm and agreeable air about him.

"Now tell me, there must be some little favor we can offer you in return."

"Now that you mention it, Tim," Charlie said, "there's this Prohibition thing."

"Ah yes, the noble experiment. Heaven bless all the federal agents. Why, if it weren't for all their alert and dedicated raids," Sullivan said, topping off his wine glass another time, "why wine and beer and the Lord knows what other brew of the devil could be sold down the throats of Americans for the mere price of it.

"I understand," Sullivan went right on, "Mr. Harding himself serves alcoholic beverages in the White House. Would you believe a thing like that?"

"Entirely possible, sir," Charlie said. "I don't know much about the President. It's my relatives I'm worried about."

"Your relatives? Well, well, well."

"My Uncle Tony," Charlie explained, "to be exact. He has a large family. He's a good loyal Democrat, and a hard worker. A family man."

"Pillar of the community, I take it," said Sullivan.

"Well, sort of," Charlie said. "More like a large rock, if you know what I mean. He had some alcohol grain from a chemical business he was in," Charlie explained. "The government impounded it in one of its warehouses. He'd like to get it out."

Sullivan drummed the table with his beringed and manicured fingers. "Well, your beloved uncle, my friend, would still require a permit of withdrawal, and such a document is granted only in the case of export, or the manufacture of pharmaceuticals. Which does your Uncle *Toby* have in mind?"

"Tony," Charlie said, correcting him. "Both. Now you see his stuff is used in preserving the relics of saints."

"The saints preserve us," Sullivan grinned. "How very enterprising. But these permits, Charlie," he added, turning slightly sober and heavy-lidded again, "they can come only from a Prohibition enforcement official."

Charlie smiled agreeably. "That's what I thought, and I thought a smart man like Tim Sullivan could surely suggest just exactly who that might be."

"It's possible, but I'll have to consult with my friends . . . Later on. Stay in touch."

"Don't you worry," Charlie said, only mildly ominous, "I will." He started toward the door but was restrained by Tim Sullivan's final words. "It's an angelic man, Mr. Charlie Luciano, who makes a gift and asks for nothing in return."

He patted his coat front. "Thank the Lord for a touch of humanity."

All the waiters bowed and scraped. As Charlie went out the door, he saw the next petitioner being tapped by Sullivan's hack to come forward and make his needs known to the great man from the Hall.

Chapter 14

Lowery's Annealing and Plating, Inc. was in the Bay Ridge section of Brooklyn not too far from the present Bush Terminal buildings. It wasn't exactly burning up the world with orders for what it did. Mr. Joe Lowery, the proprietor, was an elderly cranky man with eyes runny from peering into his various vats of viscous fluids.

He wore garters on his rolled-up shirt sleeves and a green eyeshade. On the day he was visited by the young up-and-coming Michael Lasker, Lowery looked particularly sour and sullen when I showed him my card. "Lasker, you say . . .?"

"The same initial as Lowery," I put in.

"I suppose you've got business with me."

"I buy and sell various distillations," I told him, "and I hear you've got a lot to sell, from an industrial point of view. . . ."

"*Had*," said Lowery. "But what good is it? What am I supposed to be doing with it? Government took it and put it all under bond and they didn't even pay me for it. Bang! Right in their goddamned warehouse with it. Almost a thousand gallons," he went on.

I whistled appreciatively.

"High-grade grain, Mr. Lasker. You know what I could get for that in the street?"

"It isn't *on* the street, Mr. Lowery," I pointed out. "You own it but the government still has it under lock and key, as an illegal substance. Nevertheless," I added, "I might still like to buy it from you."

Lowery looked at me sharply as if whittling me down to size. *"Why?"* he asked.

"Maybe it will be worth something when this Prohibition's over."

"Don't hold your breath, Mr. Lasker."

"So, maybe I'm a gambler, or a philanthropist," I added. "That's maybe why I can't pay you that much. I'm very concerned about my future and it's an investment. Who knows what'll happen?"

Lowery asked, "How much?"

"How much is it worth to you," I asked, "locked in some warehouse?"

"He dresses like an Arrow collar advertisement," said Lowery, "and he's just as sharp as an arrow too." He paused, then asked abruptly, "You're a Yid, aren't you, Lasker?"

"Yes, I'm Jewish, Mr. Lowery."

"No offense, Lasker, I've got lots of Jewish friends here in Bay Ridge. And in Bensonhurst, too," he added.

"So have I, Mr. Lowery."

"There's a bottle of Old Overholt left in the office," said Lowery. "Come and have a drink and let's talk this over like businessmen."

Chapter 15

Now that we had legal title to the stuff, it wasn't so important to get actual physical possession until we had our customer.

That was all Charlie's department again. He arranged a meeting with himself, Valenti, Joe Masseria, and Tommy Lucchese at Masseria's bottling plant behind some produce stalls in Little Italy.

Lucchese was the go-between, an interesting character, as I remember. They called him Three Finger Brown after a famous baseball pitcher of the time.

A regular pain in the ass, they all told me.

Valenti, as you may recall, was Mr. Goodman's brander and tormentor. He was just a walking armory, Masseria's bodyguard, and it was Masseria's produce stall that served as front for the bottling plant.

When Charlie went to see Masseria for that meeting, Don Guiseppe was eating a big stalk of grapes like Henry VIII, and spitting the seeds into an elephant-foot wastebasket across the room.

Having come up in the world meant to Masseria a definite swelling forth. He was so big and round, an elephant of a man himself, with heavy droopy-lidded eyes and thick lips, one of the last of the Roman Caesars.

Lucchese, of course, made the introductions.

"Charlie, Joe the Boss. Mr. Masseria to you."

Masseria made a little circling gesture with his finger

and pointed it at Luciano—the same way he did in the car that last time they met.

"*Maron*, Luciano baby, I ain't seen you since that time you got yourself pinched."

Charlie remained calm. "We're both different people now, Mr. Masseria."

He studied the boss's swollen face.

Masseria said, "Well, sure. We grew up. Times change. Listen, Charlie," he said, "what's another name for the Charleston?"

"You mean the town or the dance?" Charlie asked.

"The dance, of course."

Charlie shrugged. "Beats me."

"An *asset* to music, you get it, Charlie." The others were laughing too loud. "An asset to music . . ."

"I suppose that's funny," Charlie said.

"You think so, huh. You better." He shrugged. "You know Tommy Lucchese?"

Charlie averred as to how they used to play a lot of baseball together in the can with Frank Costello, and the other guys. "We used to call him Three Finger Brown," he put on, "just like the pitcher."

"Well, he got all his fingers now. You know him?"

He pushed a thumb toward Valenti. Charlie looked and remembered, of course, that evening with Valenti and Goodman, but his face showed nothing: an oil painting. "I haven't yet had the pleasure, I believe."

"Mutual," went Valenti, bowing a little.

Masseria took a big mouthful of grapes and popped them, one by one, with his teeth. "Umberto Valenti, my *paisan* and my friend. My protector . . . Everybody's my friend here, right," he told Valenti.

"I come here to talk business, Mr. Masseria," Charlie put in as if to remind him.

With the grapes thoroughly chewed and swallowed, Masseria said, "Luciano's got a proposition for us, so give him all your ears."

"*Lend me* your ears," Charlie corrected him. "That is if

58

you're at all interested in nine hundred and fifty gallons of purest grain alcohol. Right out of a federal warehouse."

"Who needs it?" Masseria scoffed. "Half the families in Little Italy, they make my mixing alcohol in their bathtubs."

"Not everybody in Little Italy has a bathtub to spare," Charlie pointed out. "You're a very big important man, Mr. Masseria," he continued. "The mantle of Lupo the Wolf covers your large frame and, of course, I am very respectful of that."

"Poor Lupo," he smirked. "They stuck him in the slammer . . . so maybe, *you know*, he could use your alcohol there."

Charlie spoke like a Roman proconsul in the court of Pontius Pilate. "You've got competition, Mr. M. Little men trying to be big men like you—Mauro—Maranzano."

"So? So what?"

"You people sell off all their home brew, a little here, a little there. Soon there won't be enough to go around. This thing's just beginning. Soon Arnold Rothstein will take his cut. Because you're A Number One, Joe the Boss, I came here to you first. You got an oversupply. Then I go elsewhere . . . *permiso* . . . with respect, *Don Guiseppe*."

Masseria eyed him balefully. "What's your price?"

"Caro," Charlie said. "Expensive."

"But *with respect*," he asked mockingly, "what about delivery?"

Charlie hesitated. "A few days . . ."

"Or you sell to Mauro. Even Maranzano."

"I sell where I want to sell," Charlie pointed out.

Masseria said, "That's some mouth you got, kid."

But Charlie knew then he had a sale.

Masseria wanted to play a hand of pinochle and talk some more, for old times sake, but pinochle and old times sake for Charlie still meant that burn scar on Mr. Goodman's wrist from Masseria's goon Valenti; and when he mentioned the name "Goodman" as somebody who was his friend while Lucchese was dealing out a hand, Valenti seemed impenetrable and stolid.

Valenti just asked, *"Cosa face?"* (What's he doing?)

And Masseria grinned when he explained, "You and me we can negotiate, Charlie. You're a good boy . . . a good son . . . We'll talk, no?"

Charlie's diary entry for that encounter is brief, but explicit:

All these Mustache Petes with their fat bellies and shark mouths will know someday they have met their master. Like Lazarus risen from the ground I stood before my Lord and Master, Masseria, and I had two mouths for him: the one said sure, and ate a bunch of his grapes and spat out the pits into my hand. The other kept to himself, and dreamed of eternal glory in this life for me and mine . . . These tedious goddamned fools . . .

Chapter 16

Once Charlie had a paying customer, it was my job to get the proper scrip which really wasn't very difficult since Tim Sullivan referred us, as they say, to Ed Fisk, a hard-pressed civil servant and a horse player with a large family.

Problems, problems. Poor Fisk had problems. But, at first, he seemed pretty reluctant—like so many other good men—to take our help when it was offered to him. Fisk called our fee, for his services, "a bribe."

"Well, that may be your word for it," I protested, "but it's certainly not mine." I figured he was trying to raise the ante a little.

60

Eventually during our conference he became convinced, and obliged willingly, if not also gratefully.

When I left Fisk's crummy brownstone flat that evening, he stood with his infant son in his arms. So self-righteous. "I never want to see you again."

Which was okay with me. I had Ben Siegel deliver the second half of his payment in a brown lunch bag to a bench in the park on which Ed Fisk had conveniently dropped a rolled-up newspaper, in which were all those necessary government diplomas.

Ben told me Mr. Fisk, like a good civil servant, seemed disappointed with his final payment.

All I can say is that stooge was lucky he didn't get a different kind of final payment from Bugsy Siegel and company.

Straight guys like that are such a royal pain, pretending to decencies which just don't exist.

In this world as we know it, the only real difference between the middle classes and people of my own ilk is we know our needs, whereas all they want to know is what other people are thinking of them. As if you could ever help yourself to anything, if you cared so much about what other people were thinking, all the time, of you.

For Bugsy, and Charlie, and me, knowing our own needs was almost always the bottom line, except maybe with some women. There, maybe, was a problem, especially for Bugsy who could get schizy about the skirts pretty easily, is one way I'll put it.

In other words he went for good girls but also fancied trash, the worse the better as far as he was concerned. In those days Ben was going with a very pretty number named Stella; they'd met at a wedding in The Bronx, and became more than just friends. Ben really liked her and she was crazy about him, loyal, and generous, nice, a real nice broad, and pal.

That didn't mean he would ever give her title to his whole life. Like kids together they often were playful, and in the beginning it was good for both of them—two good-lookers together like that; the world seemed like your dish of farfel, if you know what I mean.

Well, on the day Ben picked up those papers on the park bench from poor Ed Fisk, Stella went along for the ride, or should I say, cover. Since they were dating, it should seem like the most natural thing in the world to do.

Afterward Ben and Stella went to the zoo and stared at all the animals. In front of the monkey cage Ben asked her—she told me this, many years later, at his funeral— "Which one of these animals is most like me?"

Ever hear of such a question? Stella was a little taken aback. "Like you?" She pointed at the monkey.

Ben was amused, but it wasn't really funny to him! He was also just a little insulted.

"Because you're so cuddly," Stella explained. "That's why I think so."

"You think that's what I'm like . . . *cuddly*?"

He seemed more than just dubious. He was offended.

Stella asked, "So? What do *you* think you're like?"

Ben looked around and then he saw this big orange tiger pacing back and forth and he pointed at the beast. "That one. That's me."

"Dangerous? Like that?"

Ben growled at her. "Tiger, Tiger burning bright."

"The hunter?" Stella grinned. "Monkey face, you can't kid me."

But he could, in a way, because that's what Ben was like; one minute sweet, and the next different—explosive, dangerous.

He really got to women like Stella. They'd be kissing and he would be laughing to himself all the while, as if he'd just put one over on her for being so devoted to him. And when Stella asked what was so funny, all he would say was, "You and me, Stella, that's what," and take her hand, like Harold Lloyd courting.

That boy-girl stuff was something Ben really fancied. Guys like Ben are like that sometimes. They've only got a few men friends, and all women are for sleeping with, or they're not friends with them at all. It's a sucker bit to fall in love with men like Ben. And he had lots of suckers right up until the time he met Virginia Hill, but Stella remained his most loyal and devoted slave and pal. Always and forever more, poor thing. She just couldn't help herself. Crazy about the guy's good looks, and physical courage. In bed Ben *was* a tiger, they tell me.

And he was a tiger in other places as well. Ben drove our new green truck marked "National Export Products" on the day we went to the government warehouse to pick up our nine hundred and fifty gallons. I was in the cab with him, carrying a briefcase with those certificates of withdrawal.

Even though we hadn't given the government foreman the proper advance notice, we got into his warehouse through those vast open doorways, and then we just stood around and watched the government's employees sweating to load us up with ninety-five ten-gallon blue cans of purest grain spirits.

It was a miracle, I swear: democracy in action. We got what we came for, and we didn't even have to tip anybody for the service. As taxpayers it was coming to us in spades.

But afterward at Joe Masseria's bottling plant in Little Italy, things turned a little tense.

Ben and Valenti each checked out the count of the blue cans when they were unloaded, like the CIA looking over the shoulder of the KGB, or vice versa. And then Ben went with Valenti to Masseria's office where Charlie Lucky was already installed with Don Guiseppe.

Ben gave Charlie the high sign, the same with Valenti and Masseria; and then Charlie announced for all present, "The deal's dealt."

"Everything's like you say. Sure," went Masseria.

He pulled out an old shoe box filled with greenbacks. Ben was leaning far over the table, and Charlie reached out for all those bucks. Just then Masseria's other hand appeared, with a gun, a Waltheim .38.

He put the gun right in front of that shoe box with his

hand pointed as if to say, "Don't touch."

So Charlie froze. Tight-lipped, he was.

Masseria said, "Why we even bother to pay you, Charlie? Maybe we just take what you brought us."

They were all eyeing each other. Ben, Charlie, the don, Valenti, who stood with one hand raised near his open jacket.

Softly Charlie pointed out, "I guess I can live with that deal, Joe. You sure *you* can?"

Masseria grinned like Nero. "How you think I got to be Boss of all the Bosses? Don Guiseppe as you call me, Charlie. I kill thirty-three men. So? Who's going to stop me? You?"

"Me!" Ben was a vicious tiger that day too. He exploded. His foot lashed out at the table so that it turned over, and with that the shoe box with money and the gun all spilled over the floor.

Now he had a gun of his own in his hand pointed two inches from Masseria's head.

He kicked the other gun on the floor toward Charlie, and by the time Valenti had drawn his own gun, it was too late.

He was outgunned two to one, and his boss's head was about to be turned into Swiss cheese if he wasn't careful.

Charlie said, "I guess Ben's going to stop you, Don Guiseppe . . . with respect . . . *Scusi.*"

"No excuses." Ben said, unaware of Charlie's irony. "I'll blow your goddamned head off. You believe that, Mr. Masseria?"

Masseria's sallow face gleamed with fear and sweat, and his beady eyes narrowed and then went wide with terror.

Abruptly he grunted, a laugh, like a plea. "No trouble. Umberto," he went on, "put your goddamned gun away and pick up Mr. Charlie Luciano's money."

Valenti did as he was told. Bending to scrape up all those packets of bills and putting them in his shoe box, he heard his boss tell Charlie and Ben, "You kids, you such red hots all the time—so serious. Can't even take a little joke."

"You ought to hear me laugh at the movies," Charlie said.

Ben still had his gun pointed at the don's head, so Masseria pretended to ignore the threat and stood up a little and reached for a bottle of wine and some glasses on a shelf.

"Come on," he said, "a glass of Marsala. We forget the whole thing ever happened."

"Some other time, Joe," Charlie said. "With respects."

"With respects," seconded Valenti when he stood up with that shoe box full of money and pushed it to Charlie who said, "Give it to Ben."

Ben took the box then and backed out the door to the ramp, with his gun still in his hand.

Masseria was feeling a little less threatened. He became expansive. "That Bugsy Siegel, he wasn't a Jew, maybe I take him in—give him *his* job."

He was talking for Valenti's benefit; the gunsel had failed him.

Charlie saw the bodyguard's face tighten with rage and shame, and then he saw this hundred-dollar bill next to Valenti's shoe on the floor.

He pointed. "You forgot something there, Umberto."

Valenti stooped down to pick it up. Then Charlie added, "Like you forgot Mr. Goodman," and he lifted his shoe and smashed it right down across the bones of Valenti's hand.

The pain drove the gunsel wild, his gun hand was a dead fish. He tried to reach for his gun with the other hand but Charlie grabbed him and threw him against the wall and battered at Valenti's face with both fists.

It only took a few seconds before Valenti went out cold, and then Charlie told Masseria, "A personal matter between him and me. *Nothing personal* to you, though."

He went to join Bugsy on the ramp.

"Charlie," the don called out.

Charlie waited a second. Masseria got up and moved toward him, like an intimate, a friend. He spoke like they were equals now.

"This Goodman business," Masseria said. "That's none

of my business. You're right. That was between you and Valenti. So maybe you've done me a favor. He's been playing games with my enemies. He's not important. If I find out he has betrayed me . . ." He made a sign with his thumbnail against his tooth. "Someday, Charlie, you going to be a big man, important. When that time comes, remember your friends," Masseria told him.

They stared at one another a couple of seconds. Then Charlie said, "I'll remember. That's a promise. You wait and see." And he left.

His diaries of that encounter record:

He is the anti-Christ for sure. Turning the wine back into water again. The people will make him pay for that dearly. This arch fiend Masseria . . . he makes my blood into vinegar.

Chapter 17

That first job we took in almost nineteen thousand dollars; split three ways it was still big for those days.

Ben was incredulous. On the night we divided up the swag in my garage, he said, "It can't be this easy."

Charlie reminded him then as how he almost had to shoot his way out of Masseria's bottling plant.

We were all pretty high, just like kids. Charlie mussed Ben's hair and teased him. "Bugsy . . . Bugsy."

Then the office door got kicked open; a very tall attractive young Jewish man in a three-piece suit was standing on the threshold. Legs Diamond introduced himself by saying, "Everybody's under arrest."

Ben reached for his gun, but Charlie told him to relax and made the formal introductions. "Legs Diamond here is an employee of Mr. Arnold Rothstein. You've heard of Mr. Rothstein, Benny, so relax."

He put his gun away and then Diamond came across the threshold. "That's some nervous habit ya got with guns. Pretty soon they'll start calling you Bugsy."

Ben didn't like to be teased by strangers. "Suppose you just say it a couple of times," he told Legs, "and see how it feels to have yourself enshrined in cement."

Diamond was a fairly lethal guy, too, despite his dapper-Dan appearance, and he just ignored Ben to make a big announcement.

"The Brain himself would like to meet you guys because you're such a big success. But, er, he won't need Mr. Siegel's presence. You can see him whenever it's convenient."

"Please thank Mr. Arnold Rothstein," I told Legs, "and tell him we'll be glad to talk business with him tomorrow."

Diamond corrected me. "That would not be convenient for Mr. Rothstein." He glanced at his gold watch. "Convenient for Mr. Rothstein will be in twenty minutes."

So that was a red-letter day for all of us in more than one respect: as we say in the trade, it was the beginnings of our doings with Mr. Arnold Rothstein, and his whole *geschaeft*.

The crown prince of gambling and numbers in New York was a rich boy turned into an even richer man. His cotton broker, clothing manufacturer father would never have dreamed his son could go so far on his own steam. And on pure moxie.

The center of his operations at that time was a casino and nightclub called the Partridge Club.

It wasn't as fancy as some places I've seen, and some which I even built in Puerto Rico. But for its time it was tasteful, opulent, and attracted the best-dressed high-toned action: debs, matrons, executives, playboys. All players. There was any kind of action you fancied: dice, roulette, chemin de fer, baccarat, blackjack. And everything blazed at the same time; the bars kept pouring; the wheels kept turning.

Big-name performers like Willy and Joe Howard, and big fat Sophie Tucker with her crepe gowns kept the entertainment brassy fun, and they threw all of their own money away at the tables, too.

Going up the circular stairway above the casino, I couldn't keep from glancing down at the action below.

Charlie and Legs got ahead of me and waited for me to catch up. I told Luciano, "Someday if we hit it big, that's where we'll put it, on the right side of the tables."

"Tell all that to the Brain," went Legs Diamond.

Suddenly Charlie leaned all the way over the banister toward one of the crowded dice tables. My eyes followed his and what I saw was very beautiful trouble in the person of his old playmate, Chrissy Brennan. Some enchanted evening, as they say, or worse . . .

Only you'd have to admit Chris had come up in the world: beautifully gowned, and coiffed, she was now a classy *nafkeh*. Rolling dice for her partner, she glittered with jewels and sequins, and the crowd around the table was egging her on to make another pass. The blank look she gave when her glance took in Charlie, though, made me think she didn't recognize him.

Charlie drew back, impassive, inside his old hurt, and then Chrissy smiled and waved at him with her glittering dice hand. Charlie gave her a sign of faint bluff recognition and started up the stairs with Diamond.

I hung back, wanting to catch Chris's next move. She turned back to the table and rolled the dice. When she faded this time, she whispered something to her middle-aged companion, a guy with a hairpiece, and they crossed over to the office below to cash in their chips.

68

Chapter 18

Arnold Rothstein was maybe forty at the time, a baby face, immensely intelligent, I thought, with understated fashion-plate elegance.

He was no continental, like Legs, but a true gentleman nevertheless. Three-hundred-dollar suits in those days, I mean, and solid silk ties and shirts—a wonder boy: the Cheshire Academy and Poly Preparatory.

Rothstein was powerful and shrewd, and he enunciated his words with a formal high-toned smartness that had never been adulterated with scrupulous attention to right from wrong.

Just the slightest accent to accentuate his good manners, a slender cigar, a big desk, a leather swivel chair, pictures of pretty girls on the walls—the tsar, the star of Lindy's and a hundred other clubs and restaurants—Mr. Big Apple, A Number One Arnold.

I fancied him immediately, a man after my own heart to whom violence was as unnaturally foreign as, say, Iranian sturgeon.

When we came into his office, he rose and came around his desk. "Mr. Lasker, I believe."

"Mr. Rothstein."

Rothstein didn't suggest we get on a first-name basis.

"It seems to me there are three kinds of people in the world," he declared. "Those who never gamble, those who enjoy gambling, and those who own the tables. The mere fact that you once ran a two-bit crap game doesn't put us in the same category."

He relit his cigar but didn't offer me or Charlie one from the great silver humidor on the Chippendale desk.

Rothstein spoke at us, as if he were a Biddle, or a Vanderbilt, or perhaps a Rothschild. "I also have interests in a number of important speakeasies and the distribution of certain alcoholic products, such as liquor, and we enjoy the same relationship there, too, Mr. Lasker. Putting it on the line, you're out of the liquor business. You don't sell to Masseria, you don't sell to Maranzano, you don't sell to Waxey Gordon, you don't sell to anyone. Now try to understand that. Because if you don't, Legs Diamond and some of his associates will explain it to you with a lot more sincerity than I care to exercise in this office. That also goes for your friend, Siegel. Am I making myself understood?"

Charlie said, "You make it very clear, Mr. Arnold Rothstein."

"*Ipso facto*," Rothstein nodded: "I try. Good. I always try."

"Two of your joints got raided just last week," Charlie pointed out.

"I don't run joints, Mr. Luciano."

"Well, maybe so," said Charlie, "but Michael's got a way to lock out the federal agents."

Rothstein sat down on a couch and crossed his neatly creased trouser legs. "Are you two going to teach me about the care and feeding of politicians?"

"You still get raided," I pointed out. "When they padlock your speakeasies, that means they'll never open again. Not for you, not for anybody. You can make that work for you."

"How?" Rothstein seemed bored, but we knew he was listening intently. He looked at the high gloss polish on his nails. "Tell me, Mr. Lasker," he said. "What would you do if you, in fact, were in my place?"

"I would arrange the raids on my terms," I pointed out. "Set it up. Then let them go to court. Without enough evidence, the judge will throw them out. Then you can apply for an automatic injunction against that kind of harassment. The authorities can never do it again. They can't raid you because you've an injunction. And now you've got a license to sell all the liquor you want."

When Rothstein heard me out, he went over to his desk and lifted the humidor in his two hands and offered cigars to me and Charlie. We accepted.

Rothstein asked me, "You figured all that out?"

"He reads a lot, Mr. Rothstein," Charlie pointed out.

"So do my lawyers."

He used a gold desk lighter to fire our cigars. "But evidently they read different books."

Rothstein turned his back to us again as if to show off the cut of his herringbone suit. "Local supplies are going to dry up after awhile. I'm now buying Scotch from Canada. What would fellows like you do with Scotch?"

Charlie said, "If I had it, I'd sell it."

"Cutting it with alcohol?" Rothstein asked. "Like Masseria's wine?"

"I'd sell Scotch uncut," Charlie said. "The best in bond-guaranteed single malt."

Rothstein spun around. "You're a goddamned fool. You could cut it maybe three times . . . triple your profits. Who'd know the difference anyway?"

Charlie was indignant, in an understated way, of course. "Is that the way you run your business, Mr. Rothstein? Cheat all the people who trust you?

"Thanks for your time," he added, rising to his feet as if about to leave.

I followed suit. "Thanks for the cigars, Mr. Rothstein."

But Rothstein called out to Charlie, "Easy, Luciano."

Like he was talking to his horse, or his dog, and when Charlie stopped in his tracks, the tsar of New York said, "I'm impressed. Jews and Italians have been at each others' throats since they got off the boat, but you two seem to have worked something out. I'd like you both to try working for me."

Quietly Charlie tried to explain. "I'm flattered by your interest, Mr. Rothstein. It's an honor from a gentleman like you."

"What Charlie means—" I put in.

"I'll say it," he blurted. "Look, Mr. Rothstein, all his life my father's been a laborer, a stevedore, a night soil hauler. Smelly, stinking labor so other people could make a profit. He hired out his body to anyone who wanted to buy the work it could produce for a day's wages, and with the surplus profits from my father's labors other families sent their sons to Harvard, their daughters to Paris, their wives to Palm Beach and on the Grand Tour."

"You don't have to lecture me on economics, Mr. Luciano. I am familiar with the theories."

"I'm not talking theories," Charlie said. "I'm talking me. I don't do that stuff. Never."

"I quite understand." Rothstein seemed amused at himself—at his lack of anger with us. He seemed to have something on his mind too. "When my own late lamented father, a cotton merchant, became displeased with what I did in life, he sat *shiva* for me, just as if I were dead. *Aumein*." Rothstein glanced at the steady inch of ash jutting from his cigar.

"So be it for mercantile minds like that," he went on. "Pious hypocrites. The business of America is business. Need I remind you gentlemen of that. As the late President Woodrow Wilson used to say, wouldn't you guys like a 'piece' in our time."

"A piece of what?"

We were smiling.

"Of action," said Rothstein. "There's a shipment of Pinch bottle coming down to the Canadian border. For thirty thousand cash, it's yours."

I started to explain, "Mr. Rothstein . . ."

"I know you and your friends made almost twenty thousand in the Masseria deal. I'll lend you the other ten at twenty-percent interest. Sell the whiskey wherever you like. I take twenty-five percent of the profits. Is it a deal?"

72

"Is it real Pinch bottle?" I asked.

"It will do," said Rothstein. "And it's twelve years old."

We glanced at each other, Charlie and me, and when he nodded at me just a little bit, I nodded back.

"You got yourself a deal," we both said then.

And Rothstein smiled. "I'm glad of that because I enjoy meeting new people."

Chapter 19

On a narrow two-lane road upstate south of Canton or Plattsburgh, Charlie and I were driving slowly due south from the border in the Mack truck with the canvas-covered flatbed. It was raining pretty hard, and I'd been dozing ever since we left Essex, New York. We were just outside of old Fort Edward on route 40, the barge canal route, through dairy country, for the straight run to Albany, and as we rounded a curve, I was jolted awake by Charlie suddenly braking pretty hard.

A car seemed to be parked square in the middle of the road, its headlights blinking on and off, on and off, as if it were in trouble.

Or meant us some trouble.

As I reached for the handgun on the front seat, the lights of that other vehicle came on bright and stayed on, and then the beam of a flashlight, swinging in an arc, floated across our front windows.

Two guys in raincoats came toward our car. When Charlie lowered his window, one man peered inside and said, "Prohibition Control Agents, Argyle Center. We'll have to ask you both to get out, please."

Charlie asked, "Why?"

"Routine truck inspection," the man explained.

I asked, "You got any papers?"

"Yes, sir," he said. "Documents in the car."

He went back to his vehicle and opened one of the side doors, leaned in, and reached for something. Even in the dark I saw the sleek menacing glisten of a Thompson submachine gun mounted with a full drum of .30-caliber slugs.

"Here's our papers," the man said. And he swung his body around to face the brush and let loose with a loud trigger burst, and then another.

"Next time we bring Benny," Charlie said.

It was simply a fait accompli that we would get out of the truck and stand on the roadway in the drenching rain while the man and his pals drove away with our goods.

"Next time," Charlie said.

And I said, "There ain't going to be no next times."

I won't go into how we got to Albany, finally, except to say it involved a farmer's daughter, a roll in the hay, and a truck driver name of Frenchy.

It was a day later that we hit the city again, shaved, washed, and rested up, and then we picked up Ben Siegel and headed straight for the tables at the Partridge Club.

Chapter 20

I stood by the roulette wheel keeping lookout while Charlie and Ben went up the stairs to Arnold Rothstein's office.

I played red, the color of my rage, and won three straight spins of the wheel.

Upstairs, in his private room, Arnold Rothstein reacted with anger in his voice when Charlie announced we'd been hijacked.

No surprise to him. The *goniff*, an actor *par excellence*: "You got hijacked and somebody else has got the whiskey? Well, I'm out of the deal, and you owe me ten big ones. Is that what you're telling me?"

They sat facing each other in the dim light of a desk lamp. Legs Diamond stood behind Rothstein, posing like Napoleon at Waterloo, and Ben stood behind Charlie's chair.

Rothstein said, "That's what I get for giving amateurs a break."

Charlie said, "Some break, Mr. Rothstein. I'm telling you what happened. I didn't say who is to blame."

"Oh, that's all right then," went Rothstein. "I didn't realize that's all what you were telling me."

He picked up a sheaf of gambling markers and started riffling through them. "Do I have to teach you the aleph, base of the matter?" Rothstein declared. "Now I want it all back. Before next year, do you hear me?

"Maybe you *were* hijacked," he went on, "or maybe you

went into business a hundred percent for yourself. I just want my ten thousand back."

"I want all our load back," Charlie said. "And I intend to get it back from those hijackers, Mr. Rothstein."

Rothstein riffled his markers again, and Legs Diamond looked a little bored with everybody.

"*Who* are you going to get it from?" Rothstein asked.

"The people who took it."

Rothstein's glance was ice cubes. "Don't give me any smart answers. *Who* took it, Charlie?"

"You did, Mr. Rothstein." He waited a moment more. "You set us up."

Rothstein dropped his markers and stood up, his face like granite.

Legs Diamond started getting jerky shoulders and twitchy hands. With his thumb pointed at Diamond, Charlie told Arnold Rothstein, "If that torpedo of yours takes anything out of his pocket, it better be a sandwich because Ben here is going to make him eat whatever it is."

Diamond and Ben. Ben and Diamond: snake eyes.

Pretty soon Rothstein's cool, slightly inflected voice knifed through the tension. "All right, Legs. Take Mr. Siegel downstairs and buy him a drink."

Ben stayed put. "I'm here with Charlie."

"It's okay," Charlie told him with a little pat on the arm. "Mr. Rothstein and I will work this thing out."

Strutting like a pair of fighting cocks, Ben and Diamond kept glancing at each other sideways as they left the office together.

Then Rothstein said, "That's a lot of working out we have to do. Where in hell do you get off talking to me like that?"

"You knew the road," Charlie said, "you knew the time of day, and you also knew what we were hauling."

He got up and walked toward Rothstein, not menacing, almost friendly. "Now I already went through this song and dance with Joe Masseria. Either I get the whiskey back, or I take it back."

"How?"

"The same way *you* took it." Charlie glared. "Only we're not going to be so nice about it."

Rothstein looked at Charlie a long long time like he was evaluating certain prospects. Suddenly he jerked open a desk drawer and started to reach into it.

"Don't!" warned Charlie, his hand went to his pocket. He had a gun.

Rothstein was unmoved. His hand with the white on white cuffs went further into the drawer and reappeared with a small white business card. He gave it to Charlie. "*Bang.*"

Luciano seemed disturbed, puzzled.

"It's my tailor's business card," Arnold Rothstein explained as he came around the desk. "Get yourself some decent clothes. I don't like my partners dressing like cheap gangsters."

As they faced each other in the up-cast glow of the desk lamp, he said, "And next time you get yourself in trouble, don't go fooling around with any farmer's daughters and their boyfriends. It cost me two grand to get that one straightened out for you and Lasker."

He was grinning. "You and me, Luciano, we just had to feel each other out. Now we know each other better. So now we're beginning. If we're going to make money for each other, you're going to learn a few things.

"I already taught you lesson number one: *this is a power business.* You don't travel without power, and muscle. There's protection with muscle, and protection with cash. Use them both," he said. "Use your head. Now you get it all back. You get every god-damn Pinch bottle and there'll be no more games, not between you and me."

It was a bargain struck, anyway you figured it. S. Klein's on the Square couldn't have done it any better, once Charlie showed what we were made of.

Chapter 21

It was about that time we began to hire on a lot of new men. These were, strictly speaking, employees, not partners, not friends. I think we must have had a nose for talent, too, because some of the "unknowns" we hired on then went on to establish pretty big reputations for themselves later on.

Like Vito Genovese, for example, who, when I first interviewed him, was just a hard-faced kid from Brooklyn, without much experience, aside from a little jackrolling. But he'd heard all about his *paisan* Charlie, and he wanted to sign on with us.

"What do you *do* best?" I asked him.

"Serious work," explained Genovese, and I knew he meant *really serious* work. And I made a note of that on his interview sheet.

Functioning as the personnel manager, I was also the man who gave you Louis Buchalter, a.k.a. Lepke, and who, with Gurrah Shapiro later went on to found Murder, Inc.

Lepke was recommended by some people in the garment business. He was well set up, in his mid-twenties, and he helped out my friends with their labor problems. His kid sister was head counselor at a fancy girls' camp in the Berkshires. And he had a lot of other connections to the uptown Jewish money, such as the guy who ran the Longchamps chain of restaurants.

The only questions I ever asked was whether he'd done

any time, and he said a couple of years, in Sing Sing. Nothing serious.

I signed him on, and then he sent over his buddy, the Gurrah, a gorilla of a man, hoarse-voiced, but good-natured on the surface. I never wanted to cross him near a third rail. He specialized in ice-pick jobs and making hamburger patties with a steamroller he had on loan from one of the big uptown construction companies.

When I asked why they called him Gurrah, he said, "They always call me that, is all."

I said, "Lepke tells me you're the smartest man he ever met."

This remark forced him to think, which was very difficult for him.

"Gurrouta here," said the Gurrah. "I ain't *that* smart. *Gurrouta* here, will ya . . ."

About that time, too, we started bumping into Captain Hearn a lot, who now was in plain clothes. He always got a nice present from us, at Christmas, Easter, and even on Yom Kippur and the Jewish New Year. Just lots of Sulka ties and the cash to buy suits to match.

It was the least we could do, after all, for the motorcycle escorts Hearn's precinct would provide for our convoys as outriders.

Some of the other people we dealt with in those days were Lou (the Meathook) Nordfeld, Hungry Hilda Rabkin, Big Hershy Horowitz (later Harmon), Danny "the Dipper" Goodfellow (also known as Badfellow), and, of course, our dear old friend in municipal government, Tim Sullivan, with whom Charlie now lunched regularly, as if being tutored in the art-of-the-possible politics by that fine Irish gentleman. "Money and votes," Sullivan would declare. "Votes and money. With enough of both, tell me what isn't possible?"

He also used to say, "Never listen to any man who says my kingdom is not of this world. That may be all right for Jesus Christ but it's not a healthy way for micks like me and wops like you to think, Mr. Luciano. Puts no bread on our tables. Hell, I ain't a saint, I'm a politician. The government and me," he declared, "we're in business together."

Tim was being more honest in that statement than he really knew, if you ask me. We tried to establish as many unofficial relationships with as many official agencies as possible—like the U.S. Coast Guard, for example. They were supposed to be guarding our shorelines and harbors from the incursions of the evil bootleggers, so Ben got them to carry the bonded stuff ashore in their launches from tramp steamers waiting offshore beyond the territorial limits.

These sailor boys even gave Ben a new nickname: "Admiral Siegel."

"Sex and money, money and sex," I always said. "What else is there except family life?"

Ben sometimes had Stella wait for him at the dock in his big Dusenberg. Stella could never quite figure out where it was all coming from; especially that day he asked her to look in the papers for houses in Scarsdale, since they were about to get married: the Admiral and Mrs. Siegel.

"Whoever said I'd marry you?" she asked because Stella was still a little iffy about where all the money was coming from.

"You just said," answered Ben, and he got her to set the date.

I tell you those were the halcyon days, days of glory. A man woke up in the morning and felt glad to be alive.

Charlie met regularly with Arnold Rothstein at the old aqueduct track where the Boss went to watch his horses working out.

Rothstein was a religious clocker and improver of the breed, up early in the light mist and fog, and still very free with advice. "You're getting a taste of the power, Charlie. Now you have to learn how to use it."

Attired like a country gentleman from Abercrombie and Fitch or Finchley, Rothstein fingered the lapels of Charlie's expensive new suit like an expert, and said, "Stay out of the wars. Let the hoodlums fight. Capone and Deany O'Banion—they're not just killing each other in Chicago. They're killing it for all of us."

Rothstein peered through his binoculars at his horses, like he was admiral of the whole world. "This Teapot Dome thing in Washington, also. The secretary of the Navy, secretary of the Interior—selling the country right out from under us. I ask you who is a bigger thief—us, or Coolidge and his friends?

"It isn't right," Rothstein went on, lowering the binoculars. "Where there's no judgment, there's no judge . . . people are losing their faith in government. You know the lesson, Charlie.

"Never reach too far," he continued. "Don't go before you're ready. Stay out of the papers. All publicity is bad publicity for fellas like you and me, unless we're seen dating Dwight Morrow's daughter. Take care of your people. Don't ever fight. Just make money. Understand?" He handed the binoculars to Charlie.

"I understand," said Charlie.

Rothstein asked, "You like my new gelding?"

"I don't know anything about horses," Charlie demurred.

"You will," said Arnold Rothstein.

Once he had been a sort of dubious benefactor to all of us: now we were all more or less equals. Arnold tipped us off to the various sorts of investment possibilities in Long Beach, Long Island, or Atlantic Highlands, and Miami: stud farms, milk farms, mink farms, and clubs. I think it was Charlie who finally got us into the nightclub business when he started having eyes for Joy, Joy Osler, a chorus girl.

The first place we bought was deluxe—we had a floor show up front and some dice tables in the back. Vito was the manager. He had eyes for Joy, too, but as she was Charlie's girl, and she didn't fool around, he laid off. Joy was just very pretty, and nice, and forthright. Charlie was crazy about her, and she felt the same way about him. They were together in Charlie's deluxe suite at the Claridge Hotel, pretty much from the night we opened the club.

One morning Charlie and Joy were in bed, when Ben got the skeleton key and let himself into the suite, carrying something bulky in a box. He went over to where they lay sleeping on silk sheets just barely pulled up to their chins, and switched on the night table light.

The room was a shadowy shambles, clothes strewn everywhere, an empty champagne bottle in a silver cooler. Ben just marveled at the clutter as he dumped the contents of his box all over Charlie—greenbacks, thousands of them.

Coming awake at once, Charlie grabbed his gun with one hand and Joy with the other. He rolled down onto the floor, pulling Joy and the sheets with him, and then he saw it was only Ben.

"What the hell's the matter with you?"

"Easy come, easy go." Ben winked, tossing great handfuls of moolah all over the place. "The good life, Charlie, needs this to support it. What's the matter with this?"

Joy came slowly awake.

"Hi, sweetheart," Ben said.

"Hi, I'm Joy."

"Let me introduce you to my friend, Charlie Luciano . . . Charlie, she's a knockout."

She blushed. "Good morning."

"Good morning, Ben," Charlie added. When Joy went off to the bathroom wrapped in a silk sheet, Charlie grinned with satisfaction and reached for some of the money, riffling it between his fingers like fine blond hairs.

"This from Cleveland?"

Ben nodded, "The Mayfield Road mob came through. We're selling everywhere, and Joe Rheinfeld has let it be known through Murray Hollander and Manny Dresher they'd like even more on a regular basis."

"Great," Charlie said. "We're going to need even more help. How about checking if any of the Coney Island guys are available? Or the Purples, you know."

From then on we almost always went everywhere in convoy with either Ben or Gurrah riding alongside with a Thompson.

As good old Tim Sullivan used to sing, "Nothing like it . . . the rhythm of a Thompson gun!"

Even when I went upstate to visit Momma in the Catskills

where I had her installed at one of the best places, Kutscher's or Fleishman's or the Nevele (depending on the season of the year and who was officiating over the religious services), Ben drove along in a separate car as far as Kingston, toting a Thompson and a couple of other smaller pieces of hardware.

Ma was pretty happy in the Catskills. She got along well with all the other elderly guests, and she immediately set out to find me a bride from among one of their visiting daughters.

Mostly when I visited, we ate hearty, heavy meals together and sat on the wicker porch chairs playing cat's cradle with a piece of string.

Sterne was long since out of Ma's life. She was older and grayer, but healthy, rosy-cheeked, and strong. I felt proud about that.

One time she went on and on about a particular young woman she wanted me to meet, the daughter of a certain Mr. Silver. "Such a nice girl, Michael," she said. "Strong and healthy. You'll meet her. You'll like . . . You can't help liking her . . . A *schayna punim* she has . . . like the father. That's the father over there . . . Mr. Silver."

She pointed toward a silver-haired man in his fifties with a Forwards newspaper up against his face. He rocked and turned pages; a distinguished older gentleman.

Ma whispered to me that poor Mr. Silver was not a healthy man: arthritis. His daughter was always visiting for that reason.

"You know, Ma," I told her with love in my voice, "every time you tell me about a nice strong healthy girl, you know what you mean? You mean the girl has a weight problem."

"Michael, please."

"A rational thinker by you means cold and distant, Ma. A sensible girl means she better be because nobody would go for her as a looker."

"You don't want my advice, my golden son, I . . ."

"Stop it, Ma. I love you. And I'm glad for your interest,

now that you're such a healthy girl yourself from all the good country food and the mountain air."

"I'm not sick anymore," she told me. "I don't need all this. I've got a nice flat to go home to. All these old men here, they make passes at me, all except nice old Mr. Silver. It's not like the old days, Michael. I'm not a young woman now. I have different needs. These old men must think my son has a fortune."

"Your son maybe does," I kidded her. "Don't you like it here?"

"I like it."

"Then stay another couple of weeks. What harm can it do?"

"It's so expensive, Michael. The money. You got yourself a new car, a big roadster . . . Where is it all coming from? Tell me . . ."

"The car's from the business, Ma," I explained. "It's a terrific country for business. It takes care of *me*—and I take care of *you*."

The screen door leading out to the porch slammed and swung gently on its hinges and I turned my neck a little and there was the most beautiful young woman I'd ever seen in my whole life.

Dark with soft features, a Spanish princess or the daughter of Haroun Al Raschid, her gaze on me was tangible with interest, and then she turned slowly toward her father, Mr. Silver. "Poppa, I have to catch my train now."

"So soon, Ruthie?"

"Next time I'll bring you all the papers again," she laughed and bent low over him and bestowed a kiss on his ruined forehead, like a princess. "Just you rest. Enjoy yourself. I'll bring the *Morgen Freiheit* and Daniel De Leon's paper too."

"*The Revisionist*," sneered old man Silver.

I had my hands knotted up in cat's-cradle string and Momma sensed some change in me. I couldn't take my eyes off Ruth Silver. She was like sable to everybody else's raccoon.

Mom asked, "Is something wrong, Michael?"

"Nothing. Not a thing in the world. Excuse me, Ma," I said as I slipped the string from my fingers and went across to where the princess was standing next to her father's chair.

I went over to Ruth Silver that first day as courteous as any man could be, considering I was a man obsessed. "Excuse me. I couldn't help overhearing. . . . If you're going back to New York, New York, Miss Silver, I'm driving back tonight and can give you a lift—if you'd like to spend more time with your father."

To Mr. Silver I added, "I'm Michael Lasker, sir. Enjoy your paper. That's my mother."

Ma was startled. She couldn't help staring at us stare at each other. Next time I wouldn't be so quick to criticize her taste in girls.

There was no need for next times. Mr. Silver said, "I know who you are, young man, and this is my daughter Ruth."

"It would be no trouble," I told her. "I could use the company."

I smiled.

Ruth stared at me a moment longer, as if not quite finished sizing me up with those beautiful dark brown eyes, and then her voice was like rippling silk. She said, "Thank you, Mr. Lasker. I'll accept your ride."

Chapter 22

During the next few hours with Ruthie Silver I was like a man reborn. We walked through the woods and around the lake.

We held hands and never once stopped talking, excited by each other's company.

"We should go back," Ruth finally said.

"Why?" I asked. "They're doing fine. Let's sit here and enjoy the view." I grinned at her serious expression. "Your father's talking to my mother. My mother's talking to your father. I'm talking to your father's daughter, and you're stuck with my mother's son. So how old is the captain?" I asked her.

She shook her head. "I don't think I understand."

"It's a joke," I said. "Like a puzzle without an answer."

Ruth plucked at a blade of grass and chewed on it, thoughtfully. She was so poised and pretty for a moment I forgot everything except the urgent need to look at her.

"How is it possible to have all one's wishes come true like this?"

She misunderstood. "I think they've been planning it—for us to meet."

"We should have met last month," I said.

"What if we did?" She looked up at me, almost staring.

"I'd have known you a whole month longer," I said. "We would have seen each other in New York. We would have gone out a few times."

She seemed unconvinced so I reached for her hand and held it to my lips. "I would hold your hand. I would tell you how lovely I think you are. Maybe I'd even kiss you . . ."

My lips were on hers before she knew it, but at the last instant she drew back. "But we didn't meet last month. Michael, I don't even know who you are."

"I went to school," I told her, lying back with my head propped on my elbow, "all the way through the eighth grade. I learned the tool and die trade. I'm good with my hands. Now I deal in cars and trucks, the transportation business."

As lies go, it was only a slight exaggeration.

Ruth said, "I was seeing this older man until recently. It didn't work out. His name was Gardner. The family changed it from Garfinkel. He was such a driven person, a stockbroker. I couldn't see myself with him for life. I'm too philosophical for that so he married my best friend, Lizzy. They're happy, I guess."

"Why are you telling me all this, Ruthie?" I demanded.

"One little lie deserves another," she smirked.

She had a worried look. Had she said too much? "So now," she suddenly added, "I help my father in the produce business. I believe in God, and I believe in love. And I don't like puzzles without answers."

She looked so young and vulnerable, I felt so sorry for her. Then abruptly her laughter exploded. She rose and pulled me to my feet.

Driving home from the country late at night, with our parents' kisses still fresh on our cheeks, I said, "The ship is three-hundred feet long. It has a red funnel, twenty-two sailors, and the cook weighs one-hundred-eighty pounds. How old is the captain?"

"That's a riddle from some book, I think," Ruth said. "I don't know, how old is the captain?"

"The eaptain is forty-eight years old."

"That's crazy," she said. "How do you know?"

"Because he told me," I said. "Are you satisfied now?"

87

Ruth made a face at me. "I liked it better without answers."

"But you still believe in love?" I asked.

"I'm not so sure anymore," she teased.

"I believe in love at first sight," I told her. "And so will you, my sweet, after awhile. It's still thirty miles to the city."

In the car, parked in front of her house, we kissed in a long embrace.

Ruth was the first to pull away. "Michael," she whispered.

I told her then, "I won't ask to see you every night. I have to work with my partners. But I don't want to see any other girl either."

Her eyes searched mine. "You make it sound so serious, Michael."

"I'm a serious man," I said.

Suddenly and quickly she kissed me and jumped out of the car.

You only fall in love once in your lifetime, I think. That was the case with me, at least, and when it happened, it was a relief. I never was promiscuous, like Charlie and Ben.

Chapter 23

Arnold Rothstein fretted; he worried a lot. At the Russian baths downtown, while he and Charlie were being steamed, beaten with birch twigs, salted and pickled, he expressed his one great fear was war.

"This business with the Italians, Charlie—the Mafia thing—the old-country Mustache Petes," he said, wincing whenever he was pummeled by the masseur. "Joe Masseria is the Boss of Bosses, King of Kings, and Lord of Lords," added Rothstein, "but sooner or later Maranzano's going to crowd him. When the time comes," Rothstein continued, "when the guns go off, we stay out . . . A little lower down on the back," he added to the masseur. Charlie listened and said very little.

Rothstein was getting the full treatment on the massage table. "After they kill each other, maybe we can pick up the pieces. That goes for Capone in Chicago, too. He killed O'Banion, he killed Weiss, he's going to tie it on with Moran."

Charlie interrupted, "I'm not too crazy about this Al Capone."

"Lower down," hollered Rothstein. "Sell Capone your ideas. Sell him your alcohol, too. Deliver what you promise. But no alliances." He went on, "Stick with your friends, Charlie. Stick with each other."

When they got up from the tables to wash off, Charlie asked, "You sure that masseur speaks no English?"

"He better not speak or understand too much," grinned Rothstein, "for his own health."

But he made sure the man got a hundred-dollar tip.

Then Charlie was sent to pay a call on Salvatore Maranzano.

The Pope, as we called him, lived in a large mansion in the Crown Heights section of Brooklyn with big gray stone lions on the front stoop.

The inside of the place was dark, gloomy, wood-paneled. Maranzano, a man of fifty, was soft-spoken, cultivated, moustached, and always received his guests wearing an opulent silk brocade smoking jacket.

"Two pleasures in one day," he announced when he came down the stairway and saw Charlie waiting below, hat in hand. "A new book on Caesar and Luciano visits my home. Rome and Suetoivius. You study such things, Charlie?"

Charlie had to admit he didn't know what Maranzano was talking about. "No, Mr. Maranzano. I never went to school much."

"A true misfortune," Maranzano said. "I was lucky—my education in Italy befitted my noble family origins. I even went to the seminary. I could have been a bishop, I think, maybe more. But the world of affairs won me from the church. *Veni*," he said. "Come."

Inside the living room a log fire blazed on the open hearth. Heavy leather chairs squatted over Persian rugs. The hangings were rose and mauve velvets and brocades.

A coarse pockmarked young man stood planted like a rock in front of the fireplace, with his legs spread apart. He wore a black tie, and Charlie immediately recognized him as Scarface Al Capone. So vibrant with power, too, in the blaze of the hearth; and then he noticed who Capone was with, and his pulse quickened. Dressed for the evening, seated on the couch, was Chris Brennan. Their eyes met in recognition and each glanced away. The desire was still there; they both knew that.

Capone and Charlie did not shake hands, but as Maranzano made the introductions, "the guest from Chicago," sized up Charlie and vice versa.

"Hello there, Charlie."

"Hello, the same to you."

Maranzano said, "I'm afraid I forgot the young lady's name."

"This is Chris," Capone said. She was up on her feet and offered her beautiful hand to Charlie. "I'm Chris Brennan, Mr. Luciano." Their hands touched; their glances were subtle but frank.

"A pleasure, Miss Brennan, truly," Charlie said.

Maranzano was always the courteous civilized gentleman, and he would never directly insult a woman, but he would tell others about her behind her back.

When Chris went off to the powder room, Maranzano looked a little sour as he told Capone, "No offense, but this woman, I know what she does. She is for sale to any man.

90

Such a woman," Salvatore Maranzano added with a scowl, "should not be invited to my home where the mother of my children lives."

A pink flare of anger lit Capone's face, but he kept his voice under control. "Sure, Salvatore," he said. "No offense."

He sat down opposite Charlie. "You like my Chris?"

"I didn't come here to discuss girls," Luciano pointed out.

Maranzano waddled toward a server and brought back a silver tray with tiny crystal glasses and a big crystal decanter. He filled a glass for each of them, "To your good health, gentlemen."

Then he said, "It's important we meet. That we make this understanding together.

"This Joe Masseria," he went on, "this pig, he stops what he's doing or soon it comes to a war. I'll send his whole tribe back to Sicily. In boxes. I'm preparing my campaign. You're both prudent men. I ask no decisions now. I ask you only consider your interests. But I tell you I will make a victory. A Caesar's victory."

He saluted with his glass and sipped at some of the darkly viscous liquor.

Capone said, "In Chicago we got our own problems, with Bugs Moran. You going to help me with Moran?"

"I serve my friends," said Maranzano and gazed softly at Charlie.

"How can I serve *you*, Charlie?"

"I'm just a businessman, Mr. Maranzano," Charlie explained with a polite shrug. "People want to drink, I sell alcohol. They want to gamble; we're interested in that too. They need money, maybe we can arrange a loan." He shook his head, "I don't hold a gun to anybody's head."

Maranzano asked, "And when the gun goes to your head?"

Quietly Charlie said, "Then it will be *my* war."

Maranzano glanced at him and patted Charlie's hand as if in friendship. "I understand."

He turned toward Capone. "Al?"

"Charlie, Mr. Maranzano tells me you're bringing in a new shipload from Scotland."

"We're syndicating," Charlie explained. "Mr. Maranzano's taking a share."

Capone asked, "Who else is buying?"

They stared at each other hard. Then Charlie said, "Whoever pays the price."

"Moran?" Capone demanded.

"I'm talking to Al Capone," Charlie said. "If I deal with *you* today, I don't deal with your enemies today."

"And *tomorrow*?" Capone leaned forward, his elbows crushing his wide-brimmed hat.

"Tomorrow's tomorrow," Charlie said.

Capone smiled quickly. "How much a case?"

"A hundred and seventy-five dollars landed. Uncut."

"If I buy," Capone said, "I take delivery in Chicago. How much a case in Chicago?"

Without hesitation Charlie said, "Two hundred and twenty-five."

Capone couldn't believe his ears. "He's kidding me."

Charlie got up to go. "No joke, Al. I'm sorry we couldn't do business. Thanks, Mr. Maranzano," he said. "Good evening."

He started toward the door.

"Luciano!"

Capone was on his feet with an order. "Two twenty-five delivered uncut. Two thousand cases any label you like. If Moran tries to bite off a piece, that's *your* problem."

"I guess it is," Charlie grimaced. "Ben Siegel will see you in Chicago."

He left the house and went to his car: a Bugati with a Silver Cloud engine and super chargers, and when he started to open the front door to the driver's seat, there was Chris Brennan all wrapped up in a silver fox fur piece, grinning like a million bucks.

"You clean the basement storeroom lately, Charlie?"

"Mr. Goodman want it cleaned?"

Charlie opened the door and stepped inside and sat down and stuck his key into the ignition.

They didn't embrace; he hardly looked at Chris, but they both knew he was damn glad to see her.

"About that basement," Charlie said, "is it true you had my handsome friend Ben Siegel down there once or twice?"

"I won't tell a lie, Charlie," she said. "Maybe once or twice."

She was solid glitter to him now, but she softened when she spoke next. "I saw you that night at Mr. Rothstein's casino."

"You should have waited for me," Charlie said.

Chris explained she was afraid. "When you were arrested, I was afraid you would think it was me—who told them!"

"Did you?" Charlie asked.

Her eyes met his directly. She shook her head. "I loved you, Charlie, in my way."

She glanced away again. "And my ways haven't really changed. I know I was pretty then. I'm beautiful now, and we're both big successes. Business is terrific."

She glanced at him hard again. "Do you mind?"

"It's not my business," Charlie said. "So? What about you and Capone?"

"A little capon," she said. "He likes something on his arm. Sometimes it's me. I hear you got a girl, though, a show girl."

"Joy," Charlie said. "She's nice, and she likes me a lot."

"Capone doesn't like you, Charlie."

Charlie was startled. "I never even met him before tonight."

"He knows you're important," she explained. "He has people watching you."

She reached out and touched him gently. "I've thought about you a lot, Charlie. Daydreams and all. Sometimes I'm in New York. I work around. Maybe we'll see each other. I can help you."

"How?"

"How do you think?" she asked back with a seductive smile.

Charlie looked away, pretended an indifference while his veins were popping.

"I better go and admire some of Mr. Maranzano's books," Chris explained. "Take care of yourself, Charlie."

She opened the door and stepped outside. She glittered on the dark Brooklyn street.

"Say something nice to me, Charlie."

"Sure. I'll tell Mr. Goodman I saw you. I'll tell him we're still friends."

Chris seemed pleased with that. Turning to go back to Maranzano's mansion, she was smiling when Charlie drove off, followed a little later by two of Capone's boys in a rumble-seat Plymouth.

At about the same time I was writing certain letters to Ruthie. She kept them in a big tin box all our later married life together.

You gotta understand; people weren't so used to telephones in those days. You didn't just reach out and touch someone, you know. You wrote or came by for a visit. It was considered more polite.

I got to like the wooing by mail when we weren't seeing each other. It improved my penmanship so I would also write a good business letter someday.

I said that time, in longhand,

Ruthie, I want for you to be my bride someday in the hoary House of Israel: for us to maybe beat our swords into pruning hooks and lie down together forever then in the darkness of our Eternal Love. To have children, and a family, a nice little house with a dog, a car, say Bensonhurst or Bay Ridge, or Boro Park, for starters. Just say the word, my dark fair love, my angel, and we shall be together always . . .

She was so shy then she didn't always write back, although she accepted my boxes of candy, and flowers: a pair

94

of genuine doeskin gloves. A reticule. You get the picture.
Next time I wrote again:

> We could be together always from now on. I'll always be
> loving you, Ruthie, always forever. I kiss your face, and
> touch your warm dark hair, and want to smell the summer
> fields again of your tresses.

This wasn't exactly poetry, but it must have worked
because she wrote back immediately on a new penny postal
card just one word: *"When?"*

No denying I was coming up in the world. That one
word to me was like a million dollar's worth of advertising.
I got busy and made the arrangements . . . et cetera et cetera
and so on and so forth, as it were . . .

Chapter 24

When the going got rough in Ohio shortly thereafter, the
rough got going. We sent out convoys headed by Bugsy
with armed guards consisting of Vito Genovese, Gurrah,
and Lepke (a.k.a. Louis Buchalter, Louis Buck, and Louis
Burke), among others. Ben always rode in the first truck
preceded by a motorcycle outrider. He was carrying a
sawed-off shotgun these days; it was more effective at close
range, and he smoked the same brand of cigars as Arnold
Rothstein: *Monte Christo Cubana Chico Naturales*.

Sometimes we'd even send out a scout plane to circle
above the convoy and report down with hand signals. We

hired stunt fliers from traveling carnivals, and then we bought our own biplane.

A great time to be alive, if you made it, like the War of the Roses between Lancaster and York. But sometimes there were slipups, and once they were almost waylaid.

Bugsy had stopped at a post manned by a state trooper who supposedly was in our employ. Lieutenant Greer was heavy-faced and on the take. He told Ben the road was clear up ahead "all the way to the Indiana border."

"Yowzah," went my friend, just like Al Jolson.

"Have a nice easy ride to Chicago."

The convoy seemed to drive off and the lieutenant got on the tube and called ahead, setting up an ambush. "They think they got a free pass," he told the party on the other end of the line.

I guess he never counted on Ben's doubling back on foot and standing right in the doorway of that trooper's shack with his sawed-off shotgun.

Ben waited until he reached for his gun on the desk before he blew him all over the shack in bits and pieces.

For shame.

(It was from such indiscretions that we often had to protect ourselves. Longey once sent us a kid from the Hunterdon Boys Club, a six-day bike racer. We gave him certain little things to do. But it turned out he was also a six-day talker to the Essex County prosecutor's office. Bugsy wrapped him in Portland cement and planted him in the Hackensack River.

We had no choices, really. Years later in Florida I met the boy's brother. He turned out to be Willy Bioff's lawyer on the union deals. He told me his brother should have known better than to cross Siegel and Luciano; that from the guy's own brother, a lawyer.)

When we became really big time, Charlie rented a suite in the Waldorf Towers for Joy and himself. I kept an adding machine there, and often visited, alone, or with Ruthie.

One night while we were waiting to hear about a particular Midwestern convoy, Charlie stood at the window nervously glancing down at the lights of the city and biting at his lower lip. Joy was painting her nails. We'd ordered food up from room service and it was slow in arriving.

Bugsy was on the road; a little later on in the evening Charlie Lucky had an appointment with the governor himself. Bent over the adding machine, I calculated profit and loss. Our biggest overhead was trucks and drivers. The hooch was cheap, compared to what it went for.

I said, "We keep buying trucks and warehouses the way we're going and we'll be bigger than Standard Oil."

"Less lethal anyway," quipped Charlie. He was impatient to hear the phone ring and know that Bugsy and the boys were safely home.

"Where are they, Michael?" he demanded.

I glanced over at the latest situation map overlays on the wall above my head. "That convoy is now heading north through Michigan. They'll stay out of Indiana entirely until they reach the Illinois border. Don't worry. Benny can handle it," I assured him.

Joy asked, "You want me to call his wife?"

"No, Stella's worried enough as it is," Charlie said.

He paced from window to window peering through the blinds at the glowing city.

I looked at my watch. "You've got that meeting, Charlie. Tim Sullivan's waiting."

Charlie picked up his jacket with a nod. "I want *you* there, too."

It was more like an order than a request, I just wouldn't accept it.

"The governor didn't ask for me," I said. "He asked for you."

When he left us, Charlie said he'd be back as soon as he could.

Chapter 25

Charlie told me later that when he was led into the governor's simple pied-à-terre, that old warhorse was standing in front of a fireplace mantel: a short compact man, compounded of toughness and charm. His voice gritty with the streets and Irish clannishness, the happy warrior as some people then called him.

In Charlie's diaries he wrote:

> Irish as Paddy's pig, a whiskey voice, burst blood vessels on the cheeks, a friendly manner. Frayed cuffs when he shot his sleeves before the mantelpiece, and a gravy stain, probably lamb stew, on his lap. Plain black shoes like a tradesman. No style there.

The governor explained to Charlie that he had asked Sullivan to arrange their meeting here in this out of the way apartment, "to be discreet. I hope you don't mind the circumstances," he went on.

Charlie was still a little in awe of such a big-time politician, and as always he was polite. "I grew up in a lot worse places," said he.

"And so did I, Mr. Luciano. You wouldn't care to compare early childhood hard-luck stories?"

"I know, we come out of the same dirt," Charlie said.

"Dirt, you say. That's maybe where I came from but where I'm going is up, up, and up. I was about to explain that to you, Mr. Luciano. I don't owe you and your friends a damned thing," the governor said. "I never met you before, I never took a nickel from you, and I don't intend to. Do we understand that, Mr. Luciano?"

"We understand that," Charlie said.

The governor was suddenly genial. "Sit down. It's permitted in the royal presence."

Charlie sat; His Honor remained standing.

"I intend to run for the White House," he suddenly announced. "I don't intend to," he added; "I am going to do it."

"Congratulations, Governor."

"Wait till you hear the rest of it, Mr. Luciano. One of the planks in my platform is going to be the repeal of Prohibition. Henceforth and forever and if I'm elected, I'm going to stand on that plank. The Volstead Act's the worst damn fool idea that ever disgraced this country. I go in, it goes out."

Then he sat down in an easy chair, one long striped trousered leg lounging over the chair arm.

The governor said he wanted Charlie to have this information so he could make his plans accordingly.

Charlie expressed his sincere appreciation.

For a moment they were very formal with each other again.

The governor said, "There's something I want from you in return."

"Name it," said Charlie, his face impassive.

The governor asked, "Does that mean you'll give it to me?"

"It means," Charlie said, leaning forward, "I want to hear what you want."

What the governor wanted, what politicians always want, was more votes.

"You've got friends all over Little Italy," the governor opined. "All through the Lower East Side. You can turn those friends into delegates at the convention. I want their votes."

"To put me out of the liquor business?" Charlie snorted.

"Sooner or later you're out of the liquor business anyway," the governor said. "How long do you think this Prohibition's going to last?"

Sometimes Charlie had the same thought. We all did. The present bonanza was too good to be true.

He studied the patrician cast to the governor's face; it could assume in profile a patriarchal solemnity, in the proper light.

The governor asked, "Are you with me?"

"Why should I be?" Charlie said.

"Because," he said, "now you have an obligation to me, and I hear you're a man who takes his obligations seriously."

Charlie thought, what was really in it for him? for us?

He asked; "Can I give you my answer tomorrow night, Governor?"

"That'll be fine . . . I suppose."

It wasn't clear to Charlie if he meant it.

He asked, "Will you have dinner with me tomorrow night?"

"I don't know about that." He was fussy about his reputation—the friend of the poor, the Common Man, et cetera.

Charlie said, "I promise it won't embarrass you. It's private. Like you said—discreet. Here's the address." He handed a slip of paper to the governor.

He was being invited to dinner at the Little Italy tenement flat of Mr. and Mrs. Luciano, Charlie's folks.

Chapter 26

The convoy Charlie was so worried about got waylaid just this side of the Illinois border by a whole troop of well-armed thugs supported by their own airplane which dropped low over the route Bugsy and Gurrah were taking and lobbed down high explosives.

One of the trucks got blown up and was engulfed in flames, and a lot of the bottled goods in the other trucks were ruined.

The canvas tarpaulins were riddled with slugs.

In the end we lost a lot of men—killed and wounded, and so did they. Ben went really "bugsy" that afternoon. With Genovese and Gurrah he was finally able to outflank the hijackers and he came at them straight on with a borrowed Thompson blazing so that nobody there remained alive, and the few others in on the heist fled as fast as they could.

It was a bad day for all of us in bootlegging: a regular waste. I finally got the word to Charlie just before he set out for dinner at his parents' house where he was supposed to be joined by the governor.

He asked how Bugsy was, and Gurrah—had they been hit?

"Like cast iron," I assured him.

"Vito too?"

"Vito too," I said, unsure whether he realized what a disaster had just occurred and what he would then have to do to whomever in return.

Later Charlie told me his mother, as usual, had prepared too much food. The men ate with their jackets off in the family kitchen, bodyguards, and all, and his dad remained a little too sullen for his taste.

The governor pleaded, "No . . . no more . . . please," to Charlie's mother, but she stuffed him with veal, a pasta redolent with rich sauce, wine, cheese, bread, tomato salad, and cannolis stuffed with cream and pieces of citron.

The more he begged for mercy, the more he was given to consume.

Charlie explained, "They don't understand that word 'enough' tonight—not even in Italian."

The governor gave his consent and ate another portion, and Mr. Luciano senior said, "You are an important guest, Governor. Without you we don't get to see our Charlie here."

There was that slight familiar edge in the old man's voice that Charlie had experienced all evening.

He said, "You make me sound like a bad son, Poppa. I see my mother—it's you I don't get to see."

Mrs. Luciano extended a platter of glistening emerald and ruby peppers toward the governor's chin, "Pimentos *prego*, Governor."

He helped himself liberally even as he said again, "I couldn't possibly."

The manners of a politician are all mouth.

Abruptly Charlie's dad leaned over toward the governor like a co-conspirator: "I know why you come to my house."

"Why do you think?" he asked, playing him along.

The old man said, "You want my vote is why."

"Hey, Poppa," Charlie said, interrupting.

"You be quiet, gangster," he declared. "The governor and me we *capisce* each other."

Extending a prosecutorial finger at the governor, his guest, he said, "I already vote for you anyway."

"And why did you choose me?"

The governor believed in wisdom from the mouths of

babes and immigrants, but he was unprepared for such total candor.

"I read the papers," said old man Luciano, "in Italian, *The Voice of the People, The Courier.* Even the English papers . . . what do *they* know?

"I read about the politicians," he continued, swaying from side to side, "what they promise, and what they do. I think this way. I judge that way. Then I ask the priest and vote for a good Catholic."

He laughed; so did the governor, uproariously.

And then Mrs. Luciano plunked down her large platter of cannolis in front of the men. "Something sweet," Momma Luciano said.

The governor was fading out: a combination of hypertension, overindulgence, and fatigue—not to mention excess gastric acidity. He put his head against his arms on the table and nodded off.

When Charlie helped him on with his coat a little later on in front of the door, he said, "Incidentally we have a deal."

"I'll count on that," said the governor, very pleased with himself.

"You honor my house," old man Luciano told him.

"I hope, if I stay in the good grace of your son, you'll have me back. Good night."

He left then and Charlie was alone with his old man. "Well, Poppa, am I still such a *bad* bad boy?"

"A boy?" The old man seemed gentle enough. "You're a big man now, Charlie.

"Once," he said, "I hold you in my arms and I pray to God you grow up to be a fine man. Do good things. So they send you to prison and now you bring me the governor."

He shook his head like doubting Thomas. "Jesus Christ, Charlie, you still a bum. Run with bums, sleep with bums, fight with bums. Your cars, your money, your women. You ain't worth the boat ticket from Sicily. You come see your momma," he said then. "Talk to your momma. But not me. *Not to me, Charlie!*"

Stricken, my partner Charlie Lucky raced blindly from his parents' flat. His mother called after him, but he couldn't turn back to her now.

It would take him a long, long while before he got over his father's reproaches. In the end Charlie would only be able to wash himself clean in the blood of other men.

When he recorded in his diaries that evening, Charlie wrote:

I live up to my deals just as Christ he promises us salvation. It's my intention and his to do the best by people, the governor included. But I will never go out of my way to screw myself and M and B, my buddies. He came to me to turn bread into water. Can it even be done? A silk purse out of a sow's ear?

Charlie wasn't being treacherous. Just honest. What Charlie meant, I think, is that old Mafiosi truism: friends come and go like politicians, but the Family is Forever.

Well, we two were just like family to him, almost, Ben and me . . .

Chapter 27

Ben and Gurrah thought it was the Moran gang of "schlammers" who ambushed their convoy full of booze. But when they got to Chicago with what was left of the delivery and told that to Capone and his chief assistant, Paul (the Waiter)

104

Ricca, they were told, "Couldn't be."

Ben insisted it indeed could be, so Capone said, "Show him why, Pauly."

Still bleary-eyed from the battle he had fought on the road, Ben was driven to a warehouse nearby and when Ricca pushed open the door, there was the whole Moran gang, laid out, as it were, in bits and pieces.

"They all got sick this morning," Ricca said. "Must have been a Valentine's Day breakfast."

Tommy-gun sickness: the by now famous St. Valentine's Day massacre was even too gory and gruesome for Ben to take in with one glance.

Bodies everywhere, propped, flopped, prone, supine, and blood gurgling down a drain.

The whole place was spattered brownish red, while Ricca stood in the doorway with Ben as police technicians and detectives from the Chicago force did their gruesome work.

They all seemed to be on a first-name basis with Ricca, too. And they let him show Ben around the place. "A butcher shop, if ever I saw one," Ben said later. "The Morans had all been splintered, slaughtered, kosher style."

They came across a pair of spectacles lying about in all that blood and Ricca said, "This poor guy dropped his glasses," and then he crushed them under foot.

Meantime, a little later on, in New York, on the very next day, Ruth Silver and I were tying the knot at the Casino in the Park. Charlie Lucky was best man. We did it uptown, with a rabbi and all, and a canopy. I broke the glass with my foot and everybody screamed, *"Mazel tov."*

Ruth was a beautiful bride, veiled in white. Once she was mine, I kissed her tenderly. Then the wedding festivities began: a bash. Lots of the old families were there, Italians, Irish, Jews; a dance band and a jazz band. Arnold Rothstein and Ben did a Russian *kazatzka* together, squatting like jumping jacks, arms folded, feet kicking out to the beat of the music. Each had a cigar in his face; the other dancers cheered them on.

At our big family table was Ma, Mr. Silver, Stella Siegel,

Joy Osler, Tim Sullivan, and Senator Fish, among others. All the girls were happy for Ruth. Stella, though, said, "You're too good for him, Ruthie."

It was a joke, I suppose, but I never forgave her for it. "That's what *you* think," I said, and afterward she and I were not friends.

Tim Sullivan paid court to our parents; the *kazatzka* ended in near disaster when both Rothstein and Siegal landed on their asses. And at Charlie's table were some extremely odd pairings: Chief Inspector Hearn and Mr. Goodman, for example, and Yetta Goodman, recently divorced, with Bubba Shaw, a jazz drummer from New Orleans.

Charlie later told me Goodman reproached him for not coming to see him for a game of pinochle more often, and my ma asked Joy when she and Charlie were tying the knot and was informed, "He hasn't asked me, Mrs. Lasker."

Stella came to Joy's assistance, "They always do this at weddings. Figure out ways to embarrass you."

Mrs. Lasker said, "I said something wrong?"

Joy reassured her, "I'm not embarrassed, Mrs. Lasker. Charlie's a bachelor. He likes his freedom. I like Charlie. So we go to other people's weddings."

Then she broke down and started weeping.

Then Charlie had a drink with Ben and we all hugged like the friends we were. Ben wanted to kiss the bride, but Charlie wanted to talk, always business Luciano. "You're off the trucks, Benny," he explained. "I like weddings, not funerals. I don't want to lose you, too."

"So who's going to run the troops?"

Ben still seemed to be a little dazed at what he'd seen in Chicago, shell-shocked.

"One of our better schlammers," Charlie said: "Vito . . . Lepke . . . You speak to Michael and work it out."

Ruth danced with Charlie. She was a pretty straight girl, as I've tried to explain, and I guess she thought maybe he'd tell her what we were up to.

"I didn't know Michael had so many friends," she said.

106

"A senator too. . . . What's going on, Charlie?"

He tried to make a joke of the whole scam. "When your first son gets bar mitzvah, maybe we'll invite the President."

Ruthie said she wasn't sure whether he was serious or kidding when she told me about it later that night.

"You never talk to me about business, Michael," she said. "Tell me about your business."

I teased, "You want in?"

"Michael, tell me. We're married now."

"We try to find things people want," I said, "and then we sell it to them."

"You sound just like Charlie," she said with a puzzled smile.

The other highlights of the wedding were when all my associates carried me around on a chair, an old Jewish tradition, and when Arnold Rothstein and Charlie had their meeting over the punch bowl. Rothstein told Charlie we were moving into Florida in style.

It was a hell of a great wedding. When Charlie started to leave, Joy was on him. "I've got some business," he told her, "with Mr. Rothstein. I'm dropping him off. Then I've got another meeting."

"Will I be seeing you later, Charlie?"

"Not tonight, Joy—not for a while," he said, because as we all knew, he had a weekend date, with Chris Brennan, on the Jersey shore.

Joy was one sweet broad. She said, "Call me sometime?"

"I'll call," Charlie said.

Charlie's diary records:

Always the bridesmaid and never the bride. Poor Joy. She certainly needs a different type of relationship with a guy who can be serious, but I'm so miserable without her sometimes it's almost like her being here.

And our own wedding contract, or *Katoobah*, when we looked it over that evening in bed, promised I should provide and Ruth would cleave only unto me. So it was all strictly legal now. She was my wife. Not even in a court of law could she testify against me.

As the rabbis always used to say once a year when they prayed, thank you, God, for not making me into a woman.

Chapter 28

A couple of days after the wedding Charlie told me he was in the big La Salle with Arnold Rothstein for a meeting out in Lido Beach and Rothstein turned very grim. "Nothing's getting any better, Charlie. It's getting worse. We're in solid in Miami, but Chicago is another matter."

"St. Valentine's Day party!" He snorted, "We don't need headline like that. Death and destruction. It's a great vaudeville act. Why isn't somebody laughing?"

Charlie said, "Capone's laughing. That's who."

"Capone's got it all his own way," Rothstein said. "He's got Chicago. And we'll get the heat. All of us."

He looked a little green when he told Charlie, "Benny didn't help, you know. That massacre he put on in Michigan . . . it was the Turks and the Armenians all over again."

"What was he supposed to do, Mr. Rothstein?" Charlie asked. "It was either him or them. Was Benny supposed to stand there and get his head shot off."

"Watch him, Charlie," Rothstein warned. "For all his loyalty—and all his love—he's still Bugsy. That brain turns off and then something else takes over."

Charlie said, "I need him. I need Benny."

Rothstein said, "Michael's your real strength. A Paganini

of the adding machine, that one. The only danger there is the day he decides he doesn't need you anymore."

Charlie never had any worries about me and Ben and he told Arnold so.

Reluctantly Arnold agreed. He was such a busy person he gave free advice only once, and if you didn't appreciate it, that was no skin off him.

What really concerned him was the massacre in Chicago. He thought it had to have been the Moran gang who jumped us but when he read about that warehouse full of corpses it gave him the fear that he had lots of new enemies.

He asked Charlie if he had any ideas about who it could have been.

Charlie said he had hunches, nothing more, because Benny didn't recognize any faces.

Rothstein asked, "Masseria?"

"Masseria . . . Maranzano . . . maybe Zwillman," he said. "Take your pick."

"What's your guess, Charlie?"

They were passing this big gray cluttered graveyard in Long Island City near the ash heaps where they were dumping all the garbage for a land fill, and Charlie had his eyes on stone angels when he said, "Joe Masseria."

"We'll talk about it tomorrow," Rothstein said.

He let Charlie off at a hack stand and he came back to town alone.

The following evening when Charlie dropped Rothstein in front of the Park Central Hotel on the way to their meeting "for just a minute" because he had to "drop off an envelope" there, Arnold asked Charlie if he would keep his piece for him in the car while he went inside, alone.

It was just supposed to be a routine drop and a payoff.

Charlie waited for him outside in the La Salle.

Rothstein went into the lobby and upstairs to his suite which faced out onto the street.

He must have let himself in with a key, Charlie always said, because as soon as the lights flashed on, there were three loud pistol shots.

The great Arnold Rothstein was a big zero.
In a later somewhat more pensive mood Charlie wrote:

VIP AR. You hardly leave the world as spotless as when you entered it. I hope you don't burn in hell, but if it happens it happens and can't be helped. A man like you could have been anything. With your background: the adviser to presidents; the League of Nations maybe. But you chose your own way through paths of iniquity and now you must surely pay. I shall miss your dapper looks and urbane manners, A. R., the bon vivant ways you had, and all the smart advice you always gave us on staying alive. Pity you didn't listen to any of it yourself. This had to happen someday from burning the candle at both ends so brightly and, in the meantime, Amen. Maybe we'll meet again somewhere somehow. *Ciao* . . .

Arnold Rothstein left no will. We got the club; the rest went to a couple of show girl ex-wives. The horses were sold at auction.

Maybe a month after the funeral his lawyer who was in Proscauer's firm sent Charlie and me a photocopy of a letter in Arnold's hand. It was sort of final words of wisdom from A. R., our mentor.

Dear boys,

I don't expect trouble but just in case you should know my esteem for you, my partners, is genuine, and this is my advice to you. There are all kinds of shady characters we deal with and some of them are more honest than others. Never take a marker from a man without a family. If you're buying merchandise always give a taste first, and if you don't know what good stuff tastes like ask someone who does. Never play the Market; that's where the real crooks are. Manhattan Island is only so big; invest in it. Never give second mortgages. Don't mess with whores. If you're selling drugs, don't buy from Turks; they'll screw you every time. Finally remember there's a fortune to be made off the poor: numbers, punch boards, loans for the working man, a very good living indeed. Whoever invented banks in-

vented heaven. Start a bank somewhere, in Nassau somewhere, on the Island—Long Beach maybe. Don't play the
horses unless you need to show off. Booze is the best business right now, but someday maybe it will be cemetery
plots on Long Island, or banks, or used motorcars. Always
be prepared to diversify.

I never met a man who wasn't prepared to gamble on
long odds because we are all so greedy.

Take care of yourselves. Make money. Don't be killers
and you'll have grandchildren.

> Your business associate
> A. R.

When we showed the letter to Ben, that was the only
time I ever saw him break down and cry. He really cared,
he kept on saying.

But all Charlie said was, "Burn in hell, A. R. You really
deserve it."

Chapter 29

The murder of Arnold Rothstein was the biggest event in
gangland since the crucifixion. At Lindy's and the other
smart restaurants people mourned his passing. Legends
sprung up immediately, some of them probably apocryphal:
that he knew how to speak to thugs in every foreign language; that he was the lover of a member of the British
royal family; that Arnold had a cache of millions of dollars
in cash buried beneath the corpse of the missing Judge
Crater.

Just who had killed him and why was still a mystery; some people thought the law itself, or friends of Mayor Jimmy Walker.

Others said Brownshirts from Munich, Germany, who were brought over on the S.S. *Hamburg*. But most people on the inside agreed it was probably a gangland job.

One evening a couple of nights after it all happened, Charlie went to Polly Adler's plush East Side house. She told Charlie that one of her customers told one of her girls that it was the work of some disaffected members of the Irish Republican Army, lead by a certain Erne O'Malley. Seems they were peeved at Rothstein and the Syndicate for selling Scotch, not Irish.

Frankly I doubted that and so did Charlie. Besides he was no detective that evening; he'd come to Polly's place to see Chris Brennan.

Chris was with some other beautiful and fashionably dressed young hookers when Charlie came up to her to ask if he could see her alone.

"I thought you'd never ask," she said, smiling wickedly.

They started up Polly's mirrored stairway together arm in arm when this drunk appeared at the head of the stairs, clumsy and gross looking, with a heavy beard and a big thick slobbering tongue sticking out of his mouth, and it was none other than Arty Flegenheimer himself—Dutch Schultz to you and me.

"Hey, Luciano," the Dutchman called out.

He staggered down the stairs toward Charlie and Chris. "This is some candy store. I been up there three times already. You should try it, Charlie."

He examined Charlie's classy escort. "Who's this?"

"Miss Brennan," Charlie said, "this is the famous Dutch Schultz."

"She knows," Dutch said. "Of course she knows. Everybody knows Dutch from here up to Harlem and back. Hey, you read about Capone and Moran? It's a miracle they didn't blame me."

"I never talk business in a place of pleasure," Charlie said.

"*Dutch Schultz kills again*," he went on. "A headliner like with Rothstein. They think I did that, too."

"And did you?" Charlie asked.

"I never would hurt a man like Arnold," the Dutchman said. "All they want is headliners," he added. "I should never have changed my name. Try putting Flegenheimer in a headline." The Dutchman laughed.

Charlie had real contempt for the Dutchman, and he must have shown it, because suddenly Dutch said, "We'll talk another time, Luciano, you'll see," as he headed down the stairs.

"Any girls left?" they heard him demand of Polly as they continued up the stairs together.

Chris had news about Al Capone for Charlie. Behind locked doors in her mirrored suite she said, "He talks about Maranzano—and you. He wants to know which side you're going to go with—if there's a war with somebody named Masseria."

"Whose side does he want me on?" Charlie asked.

"Al thinks he's going to have to fight you—sooner or later," she said. "That's all I know, Charlie," she paused. "I said I'd help you and I'm trying to."

"You have. Thank you, Chris." He started for the door.

"Charlie," she said. "You don't have to leave *right away*."

"That was last weekend," he reminded her. "Hon . . . this is business."

He was going to meet me and Inspector Hearn at the Partridge Club, Rothstein's old place in which our interests were now paramount. I'd come up by limousine from my honeymoon at the Marlboro Blenheim Hotel in Atlantic City.

Hearn and Charlie had been two of Arnold's distinguished pallbearers, and they were still wearing the black armbands on their suit jackets. I must have looked odd that evening in plus fours and a golf cap, but I had rushed right to New York from the golf course without even changing.

When Charlie arrived, Hearn was on the phone to headquarters; he'd been on quite some time. We heard him say, "I'll be coming in. All right." Then he hung up.

"How's Ruthie?" Charlie asked me.

"She understands."

He asked Hearn, "What do we know?"

"You were downstairs in the car so what do you know?" Hearn asked. "There were three shots, a forty five U.S. Army standard, such as they issue to officers from warrant on up. Whoever did it threw the gun out the window. We found it near the service entrance."

Charlie was talking mostly to me; he swiveled my chair around, but let the cop overhear.

He said, "Rothstein broke up with Legs Diamond about a year ago." He turned to Hearn to give him an order. "I want to know all about Mr. Legs Diamond."

Hearn said Diamond had to be clean, since he was in Cleveland at the time of the killing. They had checked out his movements with the Cleveland police.

Just then Ben came into the room and Hearn put on his topcoat and started to go. "We'll do everything we can," he said. "You know how I and the other guys on the force felt about Arnold . . . a real gentleman . . . I'm sorry, Ben."

"Thanks, Inspector."

A mockery of law and order, if ever I saw one.

When Hearn left, we all regarded each other in silence. Ben asked, "Do they know anything?"

"Not yet," Charlie said.

"Anything I can do?" he asked.

Charlie blew up. "What are you going to do, kill somebody? Who're you going to kill?"

"Take it easy, Charlie," I said.

He said, "It's because he gets so crazy, Michael, I lose my temper sometimes."

We all three had lost a patron, and good friend. No

wonder we were on each other that day.

I pointed out, "Rothstein taught us to stay out of wars . . . let the others fight, and then we pick up the pieces. Rothstein's dead. There's nothing we can do about that and we don't want to really. The pieces all belong to us now. This club . . . the others . . . all the bottled stock. Everything. We just have to hold on to it."

Charlie paced about a moment, seeming dubious. Finally he said, "Go over the books, Michael, and let me know where we stand." He left us and went home.

"Blood everywhere," his diaries later recorded.

Arnold lost everything when he lost his life. The end of the world, I think. Foul deeds . . . as foul as our rewards . . . except now we get to sit in the catbird seat. *Will these hands ever be as clean again as they were that one time with C when I burned my mark into my flesh?*

Ben stayed. "I'm going up to Scarsdale. You want me to stay, Mike?"

"No," I said, going back to my adding machine and starting to do the current balance all over again.

Chapter 30

The pressure was on all of us now, like sticky underwear. It created fear and tension, and we just had to take refuge in old sanctuaries of a sort. Charlie sometimes spent his Friday nights with the Goodman family again. The old man owed him a lot for taking the lid off Masseria's protection scam on him, and Charlie really liked Mrs. Goodman's homemade gefilte fish with pink horseradish sauce.

Goodman was a sweet earnest old man and had often given Charlie his own version of reproachful *pinteles*—as much sweet lecture as reproach.

Sometimes he even quoted from the Talmud. "A person who doesn't enjoy all the fruits the world has to offer is a sinner."

Charlie told me Goodman had said that once when he turned up his nose at Mrs. Goodman's strong horseradish.

"Horseradish? In the Talmud?" asked Charlie.

"Bitter herbs," answered Goodman.

One day lunching in a deli, he inquired, "So? Who killed your friend?"

"I don't know," Charlie shrugged. "Maybe we'll never know."

Goodman was worried for Charlie, and he showed his hand. "Will it be the same with you, my almost son? I don't want to say *kaddish* for you, Charlie, because of some gangster's bullet from an I-don't-know. Life passes. Yetta breaks up with her husband, and now this."

"It's the life I picked," said Charlie. "No complaints, Mr. Goodman."

He was sad and he turned a little wry. "Like Benny says, We only kill each other, Mr. . . . ."

"Call me Abram," Goodman said. "We know each other long enough."

Goodman leaned forward across the table. "You think this meeting . . . This League of Nations in Atlantic City thing among the hooligans will change all that?"

"We're going to try and talk some sense into them guys. They'll all be there. Chicago . . . Detroit . . . Cleveland, New Orleans, the Boston gang. It's the first time we'll have them all together."

"And will the hooligan cops be there too? Mr. Hoover and his goons?"

"Let's hope not, Abe."

116

"Abram," he was corrected. "You'll talk sense with men who talk with guns? What kind of world you think you're living in?"

Charlie said, "Maybe we'll change the world, Abram . . . you and me . . ."

"Finish your lunch, Luciano, *mein kind*," said Goodman. "We'll go back to the factory. I'll buy you a new hat."

"Got any that are bulletproof?" Charlie smiled.

"Some joke."

The meetings were held in Atlantic City because it was still my honeymoon and I wasn't interrupting it anymore than I had to, for Ruthie's sake.

Some honeymoon, with the likes of "Little Farfel," and Paul the Waiter, Al Capone, Dutch Schultz, Waxey Hammershlag, and their girls, and their bodyguards. Bulletproof cars and bulletproof vests and luggage checks and smoke-filled suites. It was the summertime; the vacationers were thick as ants along the beaches, the boardwalk, all the restaurants. Paul Erikson was there, and Costello, too. Ben and I were the greeters, so naturally Stella was along, and Ruthie, of course.

They got to talking about their husbands, as women in those days did too much of the time, having no other lives of their own to speak of.

Ruthie said, "Does Ben like to make love a whole lot?"

"To every chippie in New York and Chicago," Stella joked, "and sometimes even with me."

That hurt look Ruth had was familiar; my mother all over again.

Stella asked, "What about Michael?"

"Michael loves me," Ruthie said. "We love each other . . ."

"Enjoy it while you can, Ruth," was Stella's advice. "I guess it's your honeymoon." Stella made Ruth sad, but she was her only female friend in Atlantic City.

They were lying out on blankets on the beach in front of our hotel, and the men, Ruth said, kept looking at them, two such swell-looking knockout girls as they were. Since

117

we were always so busy, Stella was all for going off with a couple of car salesmen from Philadelphia for lunch or a drink, but Ruth was shocked by her frivolity.

She tried to change the subject by telling Stella our plans.

"Michael says we'll go to Havana when the business season's over."

"Ben and me, we've been married almost two years," Stella told her, "and the season hasn't been over yet."

"Michael promised."

"Don't they all," she said. Stella had tears in her eyes. "I like you but you're so naïve. They're kids, our husbands, and all they know how to do is play store, with guns. Why be so blue? Do what your momma did and her momma before her. Get yourself a real fella on the side. Half the uptown women have them. Makes life worth living."

"Stella," Ruthie just couldn't believe her ears. "You don't believe any of that, do you?"

"I do, but don't mind me, honey, I'm just talking."

"But, Stella, you and Ben . . ."

At that very moment maybe fifty paces away Al Capone, and me, and a certain Moe from Cleveland in a straw hat, among others, were being wheeled down the boardwalk in bath chairs. It was a procession.

Capone pointed down at the women on the beach and the straight men taking a day off from their office jobs wearing rolled-up trousers, dipping their feet into the surf, and asked Moe what he thought of the life in Atlantic City.

"Beats Cleveland," Moe said. He pointed at his attendant, "These guys must think we can't walk."

Capone said, "Thank God we don't have to."

We all broke up.

Capone said, "You own a city. I own a city. What's Luciano own, Michael?"

"He owns himself," I told Capone. "Charlie's his own man, Al."

Meantime the fellow in question was at the other end of the boardwalk near one of the auction houses, with Frank Costello and King Solomon of Boston. They were all eating

118

ice-cream cones to celebrate the King's purchase, for five thousand dollars cash, of a genuine oil painting of Leonardo da Vinci's "The Last Supper" by an unknown Florentine artist.

Charlie said, "The King here is going to buy up all of Atlantic City, if we don't watch him."

"I'll give it to my kids," King said, "like this painting here."

But there was a certain amount of business to discuss too.

Charlie told Frank, "When we were kids in prison, you said it yourself. They got you for carrying a gun. You said Frank Costello's never gonna carry a gun again. If we use our heads, Frank, we can get rid of the guns—if we can just come to an understanding."

Hoarse-voiced, dapper, a frog of a man in a sleek gray suit, Costello asked, "With who? Everybody isn't here, Charlie."

And King Solomon wanted to know where was Masseria and Maranzano? "They spit in your eye," he said.

Charlie said they were a New York problem. "We'll take care of New York," he said. "Right now I'm looking for a national arrangement."

"I'm New York, too," Costello said. "Me and Paul Erikson are bookmaking in the city, and if I bury the hatchet, somebody just may be able to find it and smash it in my head. So talk to the King if you like."

He walked away to the iron rail fence above the beach to have a smoke.

Charlie asked Sol, "What do you think?"

"New England will go along with Capone," Solomon said.

Charlie pointed out that Capone was a killer and he was killing us everywhere he could: in Michigan, and he probably killed Arnold Rothstein, too.

"People can't even walk the streets anymore," he said.

But Solomon was like all the others: cautious and afraid, intimidated by Capone's brutality and ferocity. "Maybe so," he told Charlie, "but he ain't killing me," and then he walked away to join Costello by the rail fence.

What a pity. Those Atlantic City meetings were practically unfruitful, a failure, we said.

The whole time I was there, I felt isolated except when Charlie and I and the women were together. The others actually seemed to be boycotting us in a way; Dutch Schultz said, for example, he couldn't care less for agreements—he was doing just fine on his own. If we were having trouble with Capone, we should "try to work something out."

Worse was what was happening between Ruth and me. At Stella's urgings she was becoming increasingly nosy about things. Ruth claimed the liquor business didn't bother her once she knew we sold liquor because everybody drank it. But Stella told her that wasn't all we did. Finally I turned sarcastic. "I do what I do, Ruthie. It's what I do so you can take Atlantic City honeymoons."

"With gangsters," she interrupted.

I said, "You know those steel stocks your uncle gave you for your birthday? They were no great shakes, I assure you. They're worth about a nickel right now."

She got the message, I think. Don't ask me too many questions and I won't tell you too many lies. It's my life, after all, and Al Capone was a threat to it for certain—to Charlie and me.

When I returned from a meeting to have lunch one day with Ruth, I found a note in her handwriting taped to the dresser mirror:

I've gone off to Philadelphia. Shopping. You really don't care anyway. Just so long as you're with your damn friends. You and your meetings. What do you all have to say to one another? I don't really care, but a woman can get lonely sometimes and needs a little tenderness. Is that too much to ask for? Please don't send your thugs looking for me, Michael, as I'm not coming back.

I figured this was just a normal temper tantrum between two people on a honeymoon who were trying to get to know each other a little, and I didn't worry too much. Later that evening she called. We made up over the phone. She was down the boardwalk at the Chalfont. Next morning she was back. She looked so sad, a little wan and bedraggled.

She told me a man had tried to pick her up, a salesman.

"So?" I asked. "What happened?"

"Michael, I tried but I just couldn't . . ."

"What do you mean you tried? What happened?"

"I'm so tired." She went into the bathroom. I heard her run the sink, the toilet flush. "I thought I could take a lover yesterday and it would make you jealous . . ."

"Where did you think you were taking him?" I demanded.

"Michael, *please* don't be jealous," she said, smiling. "Nothing really happened. I promise . . ."

She looked so dark and beautiful then in the stark white bathroom light. I went over to her and we embraced. I knew she would never willingly betray me, and I was just so damn busy. Things were taking shape rapidly. Moving much too fast.

Charlie suggested we arrange a meeting with Scarface through Paul (the Waiter) Ricca, and I sent along Ben with Charlie, as a bodyguard, one evening to the Steel Pier where Capone was waiting with his own bodyguards.

The bodyguards were dismissed just as soon as Capone and Charlie got together, and then these two walked up and down the pier together.

Capone was bluntness personified; dark sullen thunder.

"You got something to say. You wanted to talk."

" 'Don't fight—make money,' Arnold Rothstein always said, Al." Charlie added, "Arnold Rothstein was a smart man."

"Rothstein?" Capone grinned. "I hear he's dead."

Exasperated, Charlie asked, "What are we fighting about anyway?"

"You and me, Charlie," Capone said, "we don't fight. You deliver my whiskey. You my delivery boy. You good. I like you, Charlie. I kiss you, huh."

"Don't play with me, Al."

"I don't play," Capone said. He squinted hard and beady-eyed at Charlie. "If we fight, believe me, I don't stand here and make love with you now."

Charlie was determined not to allow himself to be provoked. "You're hurting all of us," he told Capone. "The Valentine's Day thing, the police will move in on that one. They'll have to, and we'll all suffer."

"The police," he snorted. "Police . . . I have no fear of them."

He seemed to grow darker and more oily in the weird green light cast off by the overhead arc light stanchions on that musty pier.

The surf pounded below their feet like alien thunder.

Charlie suddenly felt a chill. He said, "We need some rules, Al—about all this killing—to protect all of us. The goose is laying golden eggs. Don't put it up against the wall and shoot it."

Apparently Capone had heard enough. He told Charlie his plans. He was going off to Philadelphia. He'd arranged through his lawyers to get himself arrested on a phony gun possession charge. He figured he'd get locked up for a couple of months and that would take the heat off as far as the headlines and the stupid public was concerned.

"*Capone goes to jail*," he mimicked. "*Capone punished*. Everybody satisfied. You don't have to shake in your boots anymore."

Charlie was dubious that it would work. "Things have to change," he insisted. "Everything has to change."

Capone stared at him dully, "Okay, okay. I'm going to tell you a story, Charlie. You think about it when you go to bed tonight.

"These two guys," he began, "they work for me and they're just like you and that smart Jew, Michael. Careful. They make a few big plans. So I make something for them too . . . a big banquet with all their friends. Then I tie them to their chairs and beat their goddamn heads in with a baseball bat."

He nodded, and laughed, a high-pitched hysterical giggle, and started to walk away, far down the pier toward his bodyguards. "Now excuse me, I got to go get arrested."

So I guess we have to say the Atlantic City convention was a failure for Charlie and me: a failure of confidence, nerve, and trust. We were dealing with paranoids, not businessmen, psychotics like Capone, in the last stages of a paresis, and there was just no reasoning with any of them, no sense of the common good, the commonweal, our mutual benefit. It fell apart also, because of Capone's envy and distrust of Charlie, and the greed and hatred of everybody else: a good try that went awry.

Bad times were on the offing afterward: bloodied times, and there were many scores to be settled. Ruthie, even Ruthie, turned scornful and vindictive toward me for the company I was keeping.

It happened the night the convention was breaking up as we were dressing in our suite to go out to dinner. She'd been holding out on me two nights in a row claiming a feminine indisposition, and when I came out of the shower wrapped inside a towel I saw her sitting stiffly on the couch, her face so pale as if she were really ill.

The drapes were drawn. She looked terrible and wan and her voice was flat, "Michael . . ."

"What's the matter, honey? You want me to call a doctor or something? You look real bad."

"I've been on the beach," she explained, "all day with that bitch Stella."

"What's wrong?" I asked. "Is something wrong? I'm sorry I've been so busy, Ruthie."

"Busy talking to gangsters," she snapped back flatly. "Those men you talk to . . . I know who they are . . . I know who *you are*, Michael."

"Whoever said I lied to you, Ruthie? I was straight."

"Like a snake," Ruth said. "It was all a lie and you know it. All your friends, Capone, Dutch Schultz, Longey. . . ."

"That's just business, Ruthie. From that I make our living."

"You make shit out of everything I hold dear," Ruth said. "I married somebody I didn't even know, an enemy."

"It's not true. I'm the same fellow who drove you to New York."

"You were lying then and you're lying now," she said. "What do I mean to you? What does anybody mean to you, Michael? *What do I mean to you?*" she asked again shrilly.

I struggled for words, to frame a reply, but not exactly deal with what she had said.

To tell the truth, it was more like I was copping a plea of sorts.

"Ruth," I said. "You're my wife. I love you. I'm guilty of that."

I bent to kiss her, but she ducked away, recoiled at my touch, averted her stricken gaze.

She was more beautiful to me, then, than ever, with the color rushing back to her cheeks, so dark and sensual, those dark eyes framed by so much lustrous dark hair.

"You'll give me children," I went on. "Maybe even a son. We'll live out our lives and make each other happy."

She seemed unconvinced; her voice remained tiny, frail, a frightened sound. "Charlie and Ben—what do they *mean* to you?" she demanded.

I had bent over her face as if to inhale her perfume and nuzzled my face in her hair and shoulders, but now I straightened up and spoke to her sharply, simply—I think, with my old fierce passion for exactitudes. "We'd kill for each other."

It was as if I had struck Ruthie with my hand. "But not for me," she said. "Have you killed? Have you, Michael?"

I tried not to lie to her but I wished not to be too cruelly blunt, "You'll understand. It isn't anything like what you think. Sometimes—we fight for our lives."

I think I destroyed something between us that day with such an admission. We were never really the same again, even after the children came. The tears she shed so easily then were for what I had so quickly, so easily, destroyed.

Ruth was experiencing all her terror of me, and my friends, and a kind of awe also. "He'll punish us," she said. "God will punish us for your sins."

She shook her head, "God help us please."

The door buzzed. It was Charlie. He came into the suite and tried to be polite. "Hello, Ruth."

She said nothing, just drew her wrapper more tightly about her, and looked glum and resentful.

Charlie noticed, then asked, "Can I talk to Michael?"

"Talk to my husband," she said. "Talk about business."

When she left the room then, she was not exactly cold, but tight, withdrawn, as she was so much of the time later. A woman wronged, I guess.

I answered Charlie's prying glance, "Ruth will be all right. We had to face some facts. I'll make it up to her."

In the pit of my stomach I think I knew even then that I was lying, to Charlie, and even to myself.

I asked, "What about Capone?"

"He won't listen," Charlie shrugged. He looked so heavy and sad, worried. Sagging . . .

I asked, "You want me to talk to Benny?"

"Keep him out of this war," Charlie said. "Those friends we're making. How good are our Washington connections?"

"We're working on them," I told him.

"Talk to *them*," Charlie said. "Let *them* handle that psycho. Do it that way."

"It'll take time," I explained. "How much time do we have?"

"Michael," he shrugged wearily, "I don't know. I just don't know," Charlie Lucky said that last night in Atlantic City as Ruth wept against the bedpost in the other room.

As I mentioned earlier in this memoir, the realization of a national crime syndicate required a genius such as I had to prove myself to be eventually. But by May 1929, there was plenty of violence still ahead before anything could be settled for any of us. In his diary Charlie noted:

So it's Armageddon. Forces of Evil versus Forces of Good. We will prevail, of course, as we have endured. I shall leap up to my God.

Make a note to buy more guns, Thompsons, and whatever else. The best equalizer is preparedness.

A wise sage once said, You can escape suffering, it isn't fated and doesn't have to be, but this escape might just be the one piece of true suffering you really could have avoided. . . .

We went back to New York, prepared to face a blood-bath.

PART TWO

Chapter 1

When you were conceived, my own mother used to say, your poor father was fishing for sturgeon in Lake Barkal.

If I wanted to, I could say the same sort of things about my friends and I and what we were all doing when the so-called "Castellammarese War" began. It was the most violent clash in the history of our industry, they say, and we certainly desired to stay clear of it.

This small-time bum Valachi had painted a whole bunch of lies a few years back in the press and, even before in Congress, about that time. Some people will say anything to save their own asses. In fact my friends and I and our associates were always endeavoring within the limits of human possibility to hold ourselves apart from that sort of messing around. To the best of my knowledge and recollection, we just were not interested directly, or involved, though of course, if you're in business, you always have to keep an eye out for the competition.

As for the rest, who needed *trouble? Bloodshed? Death?* Not us, certainly.

It was all Maranzano's doing. They named the whole goddamn war after him—he came from Castellammare, Sicily—and he was trying to unseat the Boss of Bosses, Joe Masseria. This battle of Caesars was pretty much an Italian affair, with Capone lining up with Masseria, and so on and so forth. Anastasia, Adonis, Vincent Mangano, Valachi, Three Finger Brown Lucchese, and Pete Morello were all just soldiers in those days, while me and my friends were trying, I suppose, to remain neutral, like the Swiss.

Not that we didn't have ideas; we figured we could go public and achieve this syndicate holding company, on the order of a General Motors. Unfortunately there was revolution in the wind. Our hopes dangled on the very slenderest of threads.

No doubt about it, too, Joe the Boss Masseria was the most oppressive of old-time bosses: he demanded unswerving loyalty. And in that crash year of 1929 things were falling apart rapidly. The center would not hold. It was doubtful that even he could expect a Capone to stick with him through thick and thin.

At the muzzle of a sawed-off shotgun, as they say, things are often apt to change quite a bit. Nevertheless political actions such as that, without the proper and suitable political education, are—in effect—like trying to catch butterflies without a net.

It just couldn't work, to our advantage anyway. Charlie knew that, which is why he tried to get together once in a while to shoot the breeze with the insurgents, among others, while studiously observing neutrality.

One evening in the Red Hook section of Brooklyn all of the aforementioned Masseria people were present at a get-together in a bare brownstone apartment to which Charlie had been invited for what could be called a Council of War.

Charlie came alone, except for his driver and bodyguard, Abe Reles, and straight away Gaetano Reina began by apologizing to him for "all the heavy artillery" in the hands of his various soldiers. It was one thing, after all, to waste somebody on a street corner with a sawed-off piece hidden in a newspaper, but this show of strength was not any act of aggression on Reina's part, he insisted. It was for Charlie's protection and security, as well as their own. The Maranzanos had patrols everywhere in Brooklyn.

Reina was a forceful little man, as I recall, intelligent, well-spoken, with a soft voice and a keen glance, but Char-

130

lie said that in that big bay-windowed room, scrupulously empty of furniture or other effects, with only Adonis and Anastasia, the lookouts, standing armed guard at the window, his small voice echoed and carried louder than he cared it to.

They all sat on the floor or leaned against the walls in a kind of anteroom, and Reina began by introducing Charlie to all the soldiers. Of course, Three Finger and he exchanged a few words, for old times sake, and then Reina said, "Joe the Boss, he's waiting for you."

He and Lucchese escorted Charlie toward the bedroom which was empty except for an old table and two wooden chairs. Masseria had grown thicker, and even a little more coarse featured, according to Charlie, since they'd last been together, and with reason, I suppose: he now viewed himself as the ultimate don, *Il Marechale*. When Charlie entered the room, though, he rose and greeted him with a sovereign's bestowal of a smile, as Reina and Lucchese stood by the door at parade rest.

"Charlie," he said, "tell me, what do they call a man with an eye in his ass . . . *Eh?*"

"A person of hindsight," Luciano replied. "No jokes now please, Joe."

"No jokes. Business. Okeydokey," said Don Guiseppe. "We make business together: Masseria and Luciano. Not so bad, huh, Charlie? Masseria and Luciano. Sit down, sit down."

Charlie sat. Masseria was facing him across the bare table. "You don't bring that Bugsy Siegel. That's good. That's real smart," Joe the Boss said. "Shows you got trust. In God I trust like in the dollar, Charlie, but I also got trust for you like I trust Reina here."

He bowed mock courteously toward his *tenente*. "I make him a boss. I make them all the bosses.

"*Down* with the pretty little working girls," said Joe the Boss. "*Up* with the bosses with the big bellies."

Nobody was laughing, not even his two lieutenants.

"What you looking so worried about?" he asked Reina

and Lucchese. "You think this Luciano's going to kill me. I know him . . . since he's a little kid."

They left him alone then, just Masseria and Charlie, across a table from each other.

Don Guiseppe began to sing: "Just Charlie and me . . . and Lasker makes three . . . we be happy in my blue heaven."

"Just Charlie and me . . . and no crazy Bugsy."

"We're a threesome," Charlie explained, interrupting. "We've always been friends, Bugsy too."

"*Basta*," said the Boss of Bosses. "It's not enough. Everything is going to hell . . . this crash in the Market . . . business is lousy . . . everywhere, everybody's business. Even Alfred P. Sloan he need to take a Veronal to fall asleep it's so bad, they tell me, and for us it's even worse. I got crazy people out here."

He had been talking to Charlie intimately as an equal, and my friend was listening intently, because he was there in that room only to listen, but suddenly Masseria's gestures broadened, as if he could address himself to all the slaves of the world who were kneeling at his feet. "That Maranzano," he said with a broad gesture, "he *makes* them all crazy. Crazy *wop* bastard."

He spoke with contempt. "He's crazy. He thinks he's Saint Augustine or Caesar. I don't know which, maybe the pope himself." Masseria crossed himself. "This Castellammarese War . . . who does he think he is? *Il Duce?* Vittorio Emmanale?"

"It doesn't really matter, does it?" Charlie asked. "So long as you two are so willing to kill each other."

Masseria leaned forward across his paunch, confidentially. "I tell you something like a military secret, Charlie. I got one thousand guns: Thompsons, and even Brownings, and armored cars; and I got plenty more captains like Reina . . . New York I got sewed up. Chicago is in the palm of Al Capone, my brother . . . I got more soldiers than Douglas MacArthur. So pretty soon we bury this new emperor, or pope. We dig a grave for Maranzano you could put all of Sicily in."

Charlie eyed him a few seconds before passing on Abram Goodman's advice, remembered from so many years back like it was only yesterday. "When you go for revenge, Don Guiseppe," he pointed out, "an old friend, a very wise man, once told me, you better dig *two* such graves: one for your enemy—and one for yourself."

Then he declined the Boss's offer. "It's just not my fight, *permiso*."

Masseria got real impatient, not with Charlie. "What do you think? Everybody dances and you sit by the wall and watch? The music plays . . . *ba baa baa bababa* . . . and everybody dances."

He had picked up his arms to make like a machine-gun gesture to accompany his spluttering sounds.

"Nobody sits this one out," said Don Guiseppe.

Another fellow with a mind like mine once put it, "The invitation to abandon illusions concerning a situation is an invitation to abandon a situation that has need of illusions." Like me, this other fellow, Karl Marx, was good with numbers and had once been burnished with the ritual blade. All that sort of subtlety, though, was lost on Charlie. He was being coerced into getting into a fight, and he couldn't quote Marx or any of the other sages at Joe Masseria. All he said was, "I've been around long enough, Joe, so I think I know how to take care of myself."

"You think so?" Masseria smiled and extended his pinky finger as if sipping at a cup of tepid tea. "Last night . . . last night you and your girl friend, you ate at that restaurant—Salerno's. You order the veal piccata and she has the scampi. The waiter he's on fill in—he only works there one night. Give you some service, *no?* Got a big mole . . . here . . . " Masseria pointed to his own face. "You remember the big mole he got? Well he also got a gun in his pocket. He works for Joe Pinzolo. Pinzolo works for me. I tell you this because last night, Charlie, I say two words on the telephone, you're a dead man. I got no more worries then about Charlie Lucania or Luciano . . . how you like it. . . . "

His face sagged, and he suddenly grew nostalgic. "We go back a long ways, you and me, Charlie. You king in your operation. Bring me your gunsels and guns and I make you my Number One Boss—bigger than Reina—bigger than anybody. With me, Charlie, with me you big."

Charlie was careful not to offend Masseria. "I'll talk to Michael," he said.

Masseria pointed out, though, that I was not one of them, being, of course, a Jew not an Italian.

The Boss of Bosses even became self-righteous. "We got enough problems without Christ killers—enough headaches. Lasker just ain't one of us."

"Neither am I, Joe," Charlie said. "The Mafia thing—from Sicily—the boys from this village against that town, that's not been my life in America."

"Sicily, America," Joe shrugged, bearlike. "It's all the same. Friends and enemies."

He stood up. "Next time we meet, Charlie boy, you're my friend or you're my enemy. And in the end I win. Me. Joe the Boss."

Masseria was going. Charlie would have to get in touch with him next time, and there'd be no time after that, he implied. When he left the room with Reina and the others, he asked Charlie to stay behind, with only Lucchese for company.

The two made an odd pair in that bare room together. Eyeing each other like friendly enemies, they were silent even after they had heard the motors start up downstairs as Masseria and his party drove off into the night.

Then Charlie said, "You and me, Tommy. We been friends since the slammer. Never any problems between us. Right?"

"You said it," went Lucchese.

"So? If Masseria says to kill me, you going to kill me?"

"It's a war, Charlie," he shrugged. "Everybody takes care of himself."

They stood in the darkness a long long while then, shrugging and staring at each other.

go back a long ways, you and me, Charlie. You kids in

Chapter 2

In the Partridge Club later that same night business went
on briskly, as usual. Our sort of customer had not yet felt
the Crash, and probably never would: cushioned by class
connections, cash, or trust funds, they came to our clubs
to go for the long odds, more or less for extra pin money.
While the wheels spun and the balls clicked, and the cages
of dice shuttled in their stems, a jazz band played "Happy
Times Are Here Again" with a slow drag.

At the blackjack tables in the front room were Ring
Lardner, and Scott Fitzgerald, both writers, with pretty la-
dies by their sides. The Lunts were on hand, that night, and
the actor Walter Houston, and the Irish tenor John Mc-
Cormack. Also financier Otto Kahn, Charlie Chaplin,
Peggy Guggenheim, and the rahjah of Mandropor.

A colorful crowd, as I say, in all, not to mention the
various debs, and subdebs, and marchionesses, and the
bootleggers' wives with their gigolo boyfriends.

Pretty much every night in the week our front room was
like that, like the first-class lounge on the S.S. *Titanic* as
it began to list and sink, while in the back room that evening
Charlie and Ben and I were having another sort of get-
together.

I'd just received another one of Ruthie's domestic
memos.

Dear Michael,
    If you can't be home in time for supper, don't bother.
I don't mind waiting for you; the chicken does. That's why

it's always so tough and stringy and you complain.

If I go to all the trouble of cooking you a decent Sabbath meal, I expect it should be eaten. Why do I set the table otherwise?

Michael, Michael, having supper at home with your wife once in a while is also a way of taking care of business.

Charlie had come back from his meeting with Masseria so preoccupied with worry he gave Ben the jumpy jitters when the two met near the cashier's cage where Ben had been dawdling with one of our best-looking cocktail waitresses.

Charlie said, "No time for that stuff now, Ben . . . follow me."

There really wasn't any point in reproaching Ben that all the women came on to him; he was like a bronze god in his tuxedo when he moved from table to table overseeing the action, and that's why Charlie and I had put him there out front while we stayed in the back room. But, on this evening, Charlie must have been feeling a real sense of danger and urgency because he told Ben, as they came through the door, "You keep letting your pecker rule your life, Ben, and Masseria will plant it in cement for you in the Jersey meadows."

"She made the moves this time, not me, Charlie," Ben insisted.

"Come on, fellows," I said. "No squabbles please."

I was behind the desk counting up tally sheets and Ben went straight to the bar and mixed himself a drink. As he squirted out the seltzer loudly, his shoulders flinched.

Charlie said, "I'm glad there's something you're still afraid of, Ben."

"Lay off me, Charlie."

I told Ben, "Relax."

And I asked Charlie what exactly was the problem.

"We're all gonna dance on Maranzano's grave," he said. "Guinea heaven. And you boys aren't even invited."

Ben swallowed a mouthful of Pinch and asked, "Who

says Masseria will win? From what I hear, Maranzano's beating his brains out."

I pointed out. "This isn't like the World Series, Ben."

"Oh no?" His eyes grew bigger.

"It's a war," I pointed out. "Kill or be killed."

Ben remained placid, almost social. "Want a drink, Charlie?"

"Just because we sell this rot," Charlie said, "doesn't mean we have to drink it."

He was really burning to strike out at somebody, anybody, and Ben was just there, available and vulnerable, to be his patsy.

"I must be a real big hit around here," he said, going to the bar to pour himself another drink.

"So?" I asked.

"So," Charlie said wearily, "so it's come to this. Sooner or later we're going to get sucked into this war. I don't see how we can stop it."

"But we have nothing to win out there," I pointed out.

"Sooner or later," Charlie went on, "we'll either run out of choices or we'll have to move. Masseria said it to me that way and we don't have the luxury to refuse. If we're not with him, then we're against him, he says."

I said, "We don't have to do anything."

Charlie gave me this long bleak look.

"We're not street hustlers," I said. "We're traveling under our own steam. We've got the politicians on our side and plenty of armed protection, too. The way things are going for us we're going to have more lending money than most of the banks. We're going to be in every business there is. And what can hurt us? Just so long as we keep using our heads."

Charlie looked at me as if he'd heard it all before. He probably had, and thought it, too. He looked so leaden and weary. I'd never seen him look so beat.

Quietly he said, "I love you two guys, and I promise I'll try to keep us out as long as I can."

"Which means?" Ben asked.

"Charlie's tired," I said. "Take it easy on him, Ben."

Charlie said, "Go home. It's Friday night. Have you two turned Catholic?"

I had told Ruthie I'd be home late. "Charlie," I said one last time. "Let's just remember—make friends. Don't fight. Make money."

"Live and let live," he said, "has got to be a two-way street, and right now it's a dead end."

"Not if we back up and go the other way," I told him. But I wasn't sure I believed any of that myself.

Between Charlie and Ben and me there had always been a fair division of labor. "You look after the troops," Charlie had told Ben, "while Michael will take care of the money. Then I'll take care of all of us." Well, now Charlie was pretty scared. The care of our trio fell heavily on him, and in those days he walked around enveloped in a cloud of worry. The Mafia war hung over our heads menacingly. At any moment that cloud could burst and strike us randomly with deadly bolts of thunder and lightning.

As it's been written, we must all love each other, or die. . . .

Chapter 3

Charlie had the war outside to contend with, but I still had my own private war of loving with Ruth at home.

It was the Sabbath night. When I arrived, Ruth was deeply immersed in Sabbath prayers; she had lit the two silver candlesticks her dead mother had bequeathed to her.

A black lace shawl covered her hair that fell to her waist, a thick shimmering mane. She circled the flames three times with her hands and the shadows of her long graceful fingers danced on the white linen tablecloth like gay butterflies. Then she drew her hands to her face in silent prayer. I wanted to fall to my knees, bury my face in the blue-black mass lying in the narrow curve of her body, the small of her back, and worship her as my goddess, as she was worshiping her god—to find sanctuary in her body and its warmth, enclosing me.

I called out her name, but she didn't answer until I moved toward her from behind and gently uncovered her sleek head, settling the shawl around her slim shoulders.

"You're late, Michael." Her voice was so flat.

"I'm sorry. Business."

"I'll get your dinner." Just like that. As if I were some kind of culprit being detained by her.

"I want to talk to you, Ruth." I leaned toward her ear.

"There's nothing to talk about," she said and withdrew from my touch as if I were a snake lying in her ear. I held her gently but firmly.

"We'll reason it out, okay?"

She looked at me for the first time since I came in and shook her head no. Her face was tight, angry.

"Michael . . ."

I hushed her lips with my finger, sealing off her words. "No, Ruthie," I pleaded. "Not like that. This is a night for truth. Everything happens in your god's eyes. Do you still believe I love you?"

Her eyes softened and she gave me a grave, tortured look. "Yes," she said in her small dry voice.

"Did you love *me*—before we were married?"

"Yes."

I couldn't take my eyes off her. "The night we were married?" I remembered that night like a sweet dream. She came to me with such love and warmth, it seemed like another era, another Ruth.

"Yes." She could not lie.

139

"The day after that?"

Ruth paused and I felt a sinking in my stomach. She wouldn't say a word. Finally, after what seemed forever, she nodded, yes.

"But not now. We're married but no love. Someday will you love me again?" I didn't know what I would do if she said no.

Almost in a whisper, my bride said, "I don't know."

I felt like I was holding my breath, like when I was a kid diving into the East River with a mouthful of air, kicking frantically to reach the surface before my lungs gave way and I would be forced to take the river waters into my mouth and drown.

"Then it'll be like this forever? *Forever, Ruthie?* Forever is a curse. Because there'll be no other woman. I don't run around. It's you I always wanted; you I want now. So when we're very old, maybe you'll forgive me for being Michael Lasker. And then we'll make love again? In thirty years? twenty? two years? six months? Can we start with that?"

I was begging for a shred of hope from that woman, but she would not give an inch.

"Start with it. End with it. I don't care anymore." Ruth turned an about-face, as if it were over. No more to be said. She started to leave the room with my heart in her angry clenched fists.

I couldn't stand it anymore, and I jumped up from the living room chair. "That's enough, Ruth! That's your mother talking, not you. Is that what you want? To die before your time, a shriveled wreck, eaten up by your own meanness in some flat in the Bronx? Do you want to die of grief and rage?"

"Are you going to shoot me, Michael? Get it over with. Shoot me, go ahead. You'll be doing me a favor!"

Her face was so contorted, a blend of sneers and hatred.

"Sure. See the blood?" I showed my sweaty palms faceup toward her. "See the blood there—all over my hands!" I felt like strangling her. "Whatever the world is out there, I don't bring it into this house!"

140

It was the closest I ever came to bringing violence into my house and I felt ashamed, terribly sad, all of a sudden. I told her, "You don't care anymore. Then I'll have to care enough for both of us. I chose you for my wife. You accepted me. We share the same house. We should share the same bed—for the first time since Atlantic City."

Without a word Ruth slipped the lace shawl from her shoulders, kicked off her shoes so that one flew against the wall and the other landed on the couch. Mockingly, like a stripteaser, she unzipped her dress and wiggled out of it, with a bump and a grind. A blank expression on her face, she stood there in her lacy off-white slip, pathetic, angry almost forlorn.

"There," she said mechanically. "We'll go to bed. Friday night," she added grimly. "It's a special blessing." She turned ignoring me and started up the stairs.

I watched her ascend in her slip and stockings. Her feet were heavy on the stairs. You missed your calling, I felt like shouting after her, but all I did was pick up her shoes and her dress; breathing deeply into her shawl, I drew in the sweet smell of her hair before I folded it and smoothed it gently over the chair. Then I turned out the light and went upstairs, too. The candles gathering their glow on the dining room table illuminated me on my way.

Our bedroom was dark when I opened the door. Through the street lights that filtered around the gauzy curtains, I saw Ruth naked under the covers. My little squirrel, my fawn, my rabbit. Her slip lay across the bed; like a child's dress, it seemed so small and innocent. I stood above her, trying to get a sense of her mood, but my wife would not look at me.

"Come to bed, Michael." She spoke as if inviting me to a funeral.

"What kind of a man do you think I am?" I asked her without anger.

"You're my husband." She spoke simply, as if it were a matter of simple facts. "You have a right."

"You're not my wife. When you ask me into your bed,

then you'll be my wife again." I hesitated a moment, but she didn't say a word, then I left the room and headed downstairs for my topcoat, my ears pricked for the sound of Ruth's voice, a word calling me back. Nothing.

All my senses were alive. I glanced toward the hallway and noticed our front door was slightly ajar. A shot of fear seared my body, I stiffened. I knew I had closed the door when I came home earlier that night. With all the guts I could muster, I slid toward the door and closed it.

In the candlelight I made a beeline for the breakfront and the drawer with my pistol.

Gun in hand, I glanced up toward the stairs, feeling positive that no one but Ruth was up there, and I ascended backward, pointing the gun at the apartment door as I moved up the stairs, like a robber making his getaway.

The light was on in the bedroom and Ruth had her back to me, donning her robe, as I made my way across the room. She turned, startled, as I closed the door behind me. Her eyes widened and her mouth opened in a silent scream when she saw me heading toward her—gun in hand. I realized that she must have thought I'd changed my mind and decided to kill her, after all. But there was no time to explain.

I covered her mouth with my hand before she had a chance to make a sound.

"Don't scream," I whispered in her ear. "Somebody's here. . . . Understand?" She nodded, and I took my hand away. "Wait over there," I told her, pointing toward the corner, away from the door. She stood frozen, the tears still wet on her cheeks. Then she gestured with her head, to look behind, and when I whirled around, the doorknob was turning slowly.

I pushed Ruth to her knees, dropped to one knee myself, and took aim at the door. At the same time the hatted figure flung the door open, I heard a shot, but I couldn't tell if it was my gun or his that had gone off first.

Ruth screamed.

The gunsel tottered from the doorway, toward the stairs

142

and I moved after him, ready to shoot again. He never made it down the stairs. He fell before I could get a second shot. When I saw his body, heavy and motionless at the bottom of the stairs, my gun fell to my side; I noticed my hand was bleeding.

Ruth came out of the bedroom. Shaking, her hands holding her face, her body was overwhelmed by a paroxysm of sobbing.

"It's all right," I tried to comfort her.

"Michael—oh, Michael." My wife clung to me like it was going out of style.

"It's all right, Ruthie."

"He could've killed you."

"*Pss, pss, pss. There, there, there*." She had a good point, of course, though I belittled it with comforting sounds.

"You're bleeding," she said, noticing my hand for the first time.

"It's nothing—a scratch."

I had seen this scene played out in so many movies, it was almost funny to see myself in the role of the hero. Ruth sobbed, lovingly, against my chest. My bride, my Ruth.

"Oh God. God help me—please."

I stroked her hair. "It's all right, darling."

To have my girl back in my arms where she belonged was almost worth it.

Chapter 4

In contrast to my troubles with Ruth, Charlie's problems
with Joy were problems of abundance. Joy wanted to give,
and give plenty, but there were all the usual business headaches, sometimes incapacitating Charlie. Also there was
Charlie's special little long-standing business headache:
Chris Brennan.

His diaries set down:

This is the Feast of San Geronimo. On Mulberry Street
boys and girls together, just like in the old days. So here
I am again, torn between two lovers, like J. C. Himself,
with his two Marys. One of them I treat like the Mother;
and the other is my mistress.

I must be a classic son of a bitch, but I just can't bring
myself to settle down. When you settle down, that means
your life is over, I think. Besides, who would I settle down
with? C? But she is Capone's girl...

The truth was Charlie sometimes did feel a little torn,
but never really very tattered: more like a man with too
much of a good thing. He had a sort of emotional indigestion, and the demands he had placed on himself were so
great he often grew impatient appeasing them. Like he used
to put it: "There's only one of me, fellas."

I think I knew Charlie Luciano as well as any man alive,
or dead, and for over thirty years we were more or less
associated in business as friends, and I would say that thanks

144

to Abram Goodman's wisdom imparted so early he was not of a vengeful, or spiteful, or vindictive nature. But he had a temper, just like any other fella, and when he got mad, he really got mad, no ifs, ands, or buts about that. He just had this bad temper sometimes. I've saved one letter, for example, he sent me from Sicily after the war for not being a more considerate husband.

You have a Jewish gem, a pearl, a woman of virtue, and you should respect her to your grave as the mother of your children, and not simply your wife and bedmate. You should show her the respect you show your own mother, only be a little sexy about it at the same time. If I had such a beauty on my hands I'd know how to give as well as I got. Virtue is its own reward. If I find out you're mistreating dear Ruthie, like I mistreated Joy for so long, it's going to be a hot day in hell for you Michael Lasker. Don't go with whores. If you got a little extra, give it to your wife, and if you're keeping something extra on the side, as some men do, treat her like a second wife. Believe me, Michael, what profiteth a man etc. etc. and so on and so forth, and what I hear about you and Ruthie makes me so angry I'm thinking of telling Vito or one of the others they should teach you a little manners.

Your blood brother, C.

Needless to say, nothing ever came of his threats, but that's the way he was sometimes: irate, a *shtarker*. As he once told Ben, "You're like a man late at night puts his hand in the cookie jar and don't want anybody to know he took a cookie. He wants a cookie but he don't want people to know he took one. A man like that ends up breaking the jar, or getting his hand broke, Ben. If you take cookies, Ben, people find out soon enough because there won't be enough to go around . . ."

On the evening of the assassination attempt on me, Charlie came home to his Waldorf suite and the uniformed bellman stationed outside his door, with a piece in his belt, told Charlie, "Miss Osler's waiting in your suite."

"Thanks, Albert," he said, though this was really *no* joy for him to contemplate. At some point, later on in the evening, Charlie was expecting Chris, for a *tête-à-tête*.

There were two more bodyguards he had to get by in the anteroom; Ben had assigned them to the suite on a permanent basis. Charlie opened the living room door and saw the dinner table set for two placed there by room service, complete with candles. Joy was lounging on the sofa, balancing a glass of vermouth as she tried to keep time with her unshod feet to the Vincent Lopez melodies on the radio. He knew at once that he was in for a tough evening and went right over to the console and clicked it off.

"Hi," he said curtly.

"Hi. Bad day at the office or what?" Joy was either surprised or playing dumb. Charlie couldn't tell for certain.

He stripped off his suit jacket and opened his collar and tried to appear casual and unconcerned. "Good to see you, Joy."

"You mean it?"

"I'm always glad to see you, babe," Charlie lied. "Have you just dropped in for a visit?"

"What's that supposed to mean?"

She was on to him and wary of every inflection, scanning him with her violet eyes, a momentary tigress.

Charlie wanted to be soothing, but he had business to take care of, just like anybody else.

"Joy," he said, "I don't want any spats. I've really had a bad day."

"When you see me lately, that always seems to be the case," she said. "Just what did you mean before," she sat up, "about just dropping in?"

"It means," Charlie said with patient exasperation, "try letting me know when you feel like dropping over."

"Suppose you let me know when you feel like seeing me again, Charlie," she said as she snatched up her coat and bag and ran shoeless straight for the door.

Charlie was immediately remorseful and called out her name to stop.

She stiffened, but did not move on, her back still facing him.

Charlie said she was just a little teary, too.

"I didn't know it was that way with us, Charlie . . . with you and me."

He went to her and held her by the shoulders. "It isn't, babe. Not with us. It's just . . . you know . . . these days we've got some problems. The business, and all, and sometimes I just want to be alone."

"Okay," she said. "So you'll be alone." She opened the door to go.

"Hey!"

"Hey what?"

Charlie said, "Please don't go away mad."

"Either I go, or I stay," she said.

"Stay just a little while," he told her tentatively. A mistake.

"And then?"

"We'll see."

Coat and all, he led her toward the bedroom, and Charlie says it was just great that time, the best ever, but in the afterglow problems developed between them again.

He was lying facedown on the bed, and she was kneeling next to him, her hands gently massaging his temples.

"Poor Charlie," she kept saying. "Poor poor Charlie, he's all torn."

"I'm not torn," he told her.

"Well, then I am," she snapped. "You've got me all frayed and draped across your personality, like an old baby blanket. If you don't need me any more just say so," she said flatly. "Any time you want to see the last of me, Charlie, all you have to do is say it real nice."

"What'll you do then?" he asked.

"Probably kill myself. What's it to ya?"

"Thanks a lot," said Charlie.

He tried to kiss her on the lips, but she was passive and did not kiss him back.

A little chill went through his body; he didn't want to

147

lose his Joy but he just couldn't be a one-woman man for her sake either.

Charlie also hated scenes, and he thought one might be happening any minute now if he didn't get Joy dressed and out the door.

Charlie said, "Listen, love, it's been such a long day . . . I . . ."

"Expecting other company?" She seemed slightly giddy. "I don't mind being your part-time mistress, Charlie," Joy said. "What I don't like and am not is being your doormat."

"Rules of the game," Charlie said, trying to make light of it. "Part-time mistress, you got yourself a part-time lover."

Joy was starting to dress. She was moving quickly. She knew Charlie wanted her out of the way, and that's what she thought she wanted, too, for the moment. But curiosity was strong in her. Her face clouded over and she asked, "Who do you like best, lover—me or Chris Brennan?"

The shadow that must have crossed Charlie's face was as much from calculation as worry, but he had an answer for her, finally, "I like you because you're here, Joy."

"Am I?" She was wistful.

Tears in her eyes; tears on her pillow, too, as if something that was and might have been had changed now utterly between her and Charlie, was altered, almost beyond recognition, by this new hurt he'd just administered to her.

Though they stayed together in the months and years that followed, the fact is they were now so very different from each other, and this new knowledge he had given her could only make the old hurts fester worse.

It was like she herself was told not to care any more, when she couldn't stop so easily because she did care.

In later years I was to hear of strange weird scenes between Joy and Chris when they met finally face-to-face and even became friends and admirers of sorts (lovers, you might say, to put it bluntly). But in those days Joy was vulnerable. And Charlie was making himself vulnerable because of the hurt he'd been causing her.

148

While Charlie and Joy were exchanging accusing glances, as if both were inside the same ice cube, I happened to call for the third time that evening to tell Charlie of the attempt on my life. All Charlie could ask was, "You all right, Michael—all right?"

Like I had just told him I had a headache, or something. Joy was in the john, I suppose, fixing her face, and when I assured Charlie of my continued well-being, he told me to get Hearn and he and Ben would be at my place just as soon as they could.

Chapter 5

Ben found out the news when he got up to Scarsdale from the club with lipstick all over his underwear.

Stella was pregnant and very, very suspicious of his every move, as she had a right to be, for Ben was chippying around again, more than his share.

More than any sane man's share, I suppose. He was just playing around twenty-four hours a day, when he wasn't working for us. And it was getting to Stella who talked about adultery but pretty much kept to herself now that she was very pregnant. When Ben came home that night to their fabulous Scarsdale mansion, Stella was sitting on the easy chair with a copy of *Your Baby and Mine*.

"Hello *dere*," he said like a vaudeville act. He went over to his wife's chair and gently placed a hand against her stomach as he always did on coming home. Ben asked, "How's what's-his-name?"

Mildly Stella replied, "Where've you been, my fine-feathered. . . "

"The office . . . with Charles. . . "

"Not on our lives," she crooned. "Charlie just called you. An emergency. He's been trying to reach you."

Caught again, Ben stiffened and pulled himself slowly back from her chair. "Hey now, what's this?" he demanded. "What are you running here—a detective bureau?"

Evenly Stella reprimanded him like a gentle friend, his wife, his mistress, and one true love. "Ben, you made me this princess. Gave me this house, the maids, anything I could ever want, you gave to me from what you do. But if you're going to lie to me, lie better than that please. At least let me pretend to myself that you're not sleeping all over town."

Struck by her gentleness, he told her, "Stella . . . Stella . . . Stella, please." The eyes pleaded with her; he drew her hand to his lips and kissed it.

Ben lied like the trooper he really was, "I swear on our baby I will never do this again."

"That's much better," she said. "Now you see, I can pretend. . . . So go call your boyfriend Charlie. Because somebody just tried to kill Michael Lasker."

When he thought about it afterward, some time later, Ben said his first thought was how could he be in bed with some dame while Mike's life was in danger?

Frankly I think this was one of Ben's "sincerities." He meant well, wished it were true, hoped it was, but it really wasn't. Ben was a creature of impulse; if a woman beckoned to him, he'd betray his friend for as long as it took to have a good time.

When the three of us were together, at last, that night, Charlie, not Ben, was the man I looked to for compassion and solace. He asked me, "How did Ruth take it?"

What could I say? That she was afraid for us and in a way that somehow helped us get through something together?

I didn't feel I wanted to talk about it, so I simply told

him the police doctor had given Ruth something to make her sleep.

Suddenly Charlie slammed his hand against his thigh, "Goddamn lunatics!"

He whirled on Ben. "In his own house, Benny! Where the hell were you?"

"What was I supposed to do," Ben protested, "stand outside with a gun?"

The two were close to a brawl. "Well, somebody should have been there!"

"I didn't think they'd try to hit Michael," Ben said. "He's not in our end of the business."

Charlie demanded, "What end of the business were you in tonight, Ben? *Whose?*"

"None of your business!" Ben snapped back, his eyes glazing over.

I intervened. "He's right, Charlie. Be reasonable. It's nobody's fault."

"You just saw how right he is," Charlie said. He ordered Ben to guard my house from now on, twenty-four hours a day. Charlie said, "Buy the house across the street. Buy up the whole block. Just do your job!"

"All right, Charlie." Ben was facing me with grave solemnity. "I'll put my hands in the fire before it happens again."

Maybe, though, it was a little too late for such vows. Charlie no longer trusted Ben quite as he had before. Other gunsels would move up to take Ben's place as Charlie's strong right arm.

Even today, with my own death a sure thing in the not-too-distant future, I can still experience the metallic taste of my fear that evening.

Charlie had sent Vito Genovese to the police morgue to find out who my would-be assassin was. When the doorbell rang, meaning Vito was back with his report, Charlie sent Ben, like an errand boy, to let him in. And then, alone with me, Charlie touched my face with his hand, a gentle, loving gesture, and said, "From now on you carry a gun."

"A man with a gun on his person is looking to be shot," I said. "I'll keep mine in the drawer like tonight."

"You'll carry a gun," Charlie insisted, and it was true, over the years, from then on. I did: a one-shot derringer, and then a .38, and more recently in my attaché case a little Uzi, with a detachable stock. It just became second nature with me to have a weapon around, but I never used any of them again, except once on a camping trip in the Rockies with my grandchildren, against some marauding bears.

So that was the evening I became the prophet armed, or should I say, armed profit. Such a long long time ago it was before anybody had even heard of Michael Lasker in the press, or elsewhere, like they do nowadays, wherever you look.

It was that same evening that Vito, returning, confirmed for us that my assassin had been Doc Calvelli who belonged to Joe the Boss.

I saw Charlie's face harden like ice. "Masseria."

Genovese repeated the name.

Charlie turned to me with raw bitterness, "Are we still going to stay out of the war, Michael? Still going to do that little trick?"

"Charlie, Charlie," I pleaded. "Where's the profit for us? Are you going to take revenge to the bank? How do I put it on the books? A credit? Do we maybe tear up everything we've ever built for this?"

He grabbed my bandaged hand. "If we don't, they'll do it again and again until they've gotten one of us. Don't you understand, Michael? It's a matter of deterrence."

"I see revenge on your face, not deterrence, Charlie."

He pouted and looked grim. Then slowly he spoke to me, with patient exactitude. "The meeting with Masseria— I said I'd talk it over with you. He said you aren't one of us. He's right about that, Michael," Charlie said. "You're really not. You appease."

"If you mean I don't make war, I . . ."

"Appease," Charlie said. "Staying clear of the war's going to make it into a war on us."

He said I was out of it then; Vito and he would handle

the war, and Ben, who had come back into the room, was now simply my bodyguard again, for the moment.

Charlie told him, "Don't make a mess of this assignment, Ben."

"I'll take care of it, Charlie," he assured us.

Still Luciano remained angry and sarcastic. "Just so long as it don't interfere with your love life, Ben old pal of mine."

Then he and Vito left us, and I kept thinking about what Charlie had said. Prior to then I'd always seen him as a man of peace, but now I saw him for what he was, a soldier, just like so many others, and my near murder had frightened him into action.

Many years later in Israel I witnessed the same kind of behavior. The young Sabras I met would say why wait for the PLO to pick us off one by one? We'll raid their bases in Lebanon, and maybe even elsewhere, before they can plan their next moves against us.

So it was with Charlie that evening, a long time ago. The worst I could imagine was just about to happen and I could do nothing to stop the butchery which surely would ensue. Still and all I tried to remain loyal to Charlie.

When Ben sat down by my side, he said, "You know how I still feel about you Michael . . . and about what happened . . ."

"It's okay, Benny," I told him. "You couldn't help yourself."

"Don't patronize, Mike," he said. Bluntly Ben added, "Charlie's going to leave us hanging by our thumbs."

"Charlie's going to do what's best for all of us," I corrected him. "I don't want to hear anything else."

Ben couldn't be contrite. "It's been your brains and my muscle all along. It's always been that way, Mike. Don't you remember?"

"Good night, my friend Ben," I told him. "This conversation's now over."

He stood there as if hoping to talk to me again, so I said, "Ben, get your coat and turn out the lights."

Then I headed up the stairs to Ruth.

Chapter 6

It has been said men do exactly what they have to do, but sometimes they also do what they've been forced into doing. You put enough pressure on the stuck door and it gives; the lock breaks, the door crumbles, your enemy flees the confrontations of your force.

That's just the way of the world. The way it's always been, since Cain and Abel.

Charlie's next move was to use Vito as his escort and pay a call on Salvatore Maranzano at his closely guarded Staten Island estate.

Maranzano's recent gangland successes had led to certain excesses of life-style and display. He lived in a turreted Victorian stone castle on fifty acres of woodlands overlooking the Arthur Kill.

It was the kind of place damsels in distress were once rescued from.

Guarded by the likes of Vincent Mangano, Maranzano existed in genuine Oriental splendor. His library was exquisite: a composition of fine rosewood and mahogany veneers, old leathers and velvet, with gilt bindings, and a collection of first editions with Fore-edge decorations. The man had set himself up as a competing Emperor of Crime. When Charlie was ushered in to see him, Don Maranzano was sitting by the window reading from an antique volume as the brilliant early twilight flooded his pages.

Charlie greeted him, as always, with a show of respect.

"Don Maranzano, it's a privilege to see you in your new mansion like this."

Maranzano gazed up with soft blue eyes and a distant look and quoted to him from what he was reading in Dante: "*Nessun maggiore dolore*, Charlie. It says here, the poet tells us, How we remember our pain in happy times . . . it's true, *no*?"

"It's true," Charlie whispered.

"Dante is so beautiful," Maranzano said. "But you should buy a copy of Caesar's campaigns and read them. Learn Latin and get the wisdom in Caesar's own words."

He removed his spectacles and put the book aside on the bench by the leaded casement window next to him. "Caesar whispers into my ear—and maybe you stand by my side. Then we take the world together."

Maranzano came to Charlie and finally extended his arm for a handshake. "Thank you for paying me this visit."

"I appreciate the invitation," Charlie said.

Maranzano turned about like a Roman before the multitudes and sat himself down on the couch, a senator, at very least, arms stretched on either side of his body like a statue. Then he squinted hard, as if threading Charlie through a needle's eye.

"For those with the eyes to see," he said, "my own campaign already is won."

"Is that why," Charlie asked, "Capone went with Masseria?"

Maranzano blinked but was undaunted. "In the end Capone, like all the rest, will pay his share of the tribute. They'll all pay, the ones who live. Those who join me, they shall share. As it has been set down since the most ancient of days . . ."

"What about present days, Don?" Charlie asked.

And Maranzano asked back, "You've met with Masseria?"

Charlie's face was impassive as he answered, "*Si*."

"Good. So there will be truth between you and me."

"My very thought," said Charlie.

155

"Joe the Boss is a boss of pigs," Maranzano declared. "A boss of nothing. We'll just leave him the North Pole."

He pushed his face into the air between him and Charlie as if it had been wreathed with olive branches. "He offered to make you a big man. You already big, Luciano. You think I don't know that? Why do I court you like a bride? Will you hear my offer, Charlie?"

Charlie said, "I'm a guest in your house."

"Everything you have, you keep. Everything," went Maranzano. "I ask nothing. Everything I have—I give you a portion. The work of my lifetime belongs to you. What we make together, we divide reasonable. This I offer you to stand with me."

It was a compelling deal; if not quite once in a lifetime, it was certainly compelling, especially when you knew Maranzano was prepared to take your life, if you welched on him, but all Charlie said in reply was, "Your offer is very generous."

Maranzano spoke back magisterially, "I will take profit from your great strength; even more after we make our victory."

"And if I still choose to stand alone?"

"Alone is a lonely place, alone, Charlie. There are many, many considerations. Come."

Maranzano led Charlie out of the library and across the foyer to the living room, with its hangings of dark mauve silk and shot satin. Two men were seated there, with their hats in their laps, and their topcoats still on, and Charlie recognized them immediately: Gaetano Reina and Tommy Lucchese.

Reina spoke first. "No surprises in the world, are there, Charlie?"

"None," whispered Luciano.

Maranzano said, "You know Mr. Gaetano Reina—the *capo* from the camp of Joe the Boss . . ."

"More than just capo," said Charlie, still whispering. He turned toward Lucchese, "*Et tu,* Tommy?"

"Me too, Charlie," said Lucchese. "We're coming over. We're bringing all our shooters."

"*Quando?*"

Reina answered Charlie's question. "When Don Maranzano gives us the word. Till then we stay with Masseria. He's going nuts, Charlie, *miseria mia*. Just like an orange he squeezes us. Business is going down the toilet and every week he wants more."

"Just like he eats," Lucchese added. "That's just how he deals with us. There's never enough. *Fongool*."

Maranzano chose a cigar for himself from a fancy Florentine humidor of veneered woods with a family crest—a fool's cap, an olive wreath, crossed halberds. He rolled it around on his lips to wet the end, a long thin cheroot of very high quality. Then he said, "These two *barones* are my secret ambassadors. But there are also others: Carlo Volpone, Angie Agrimonte, Vince Rugoloso, you know, types like that: Minor vassals, Charlie, to their liege lord, namely me, Maranzano.

"I think of it as a matter of diplomacy," he went on. "Diplomacy, Charlie, and the force of arms. To be wise and ruthless. Who can resist us?"

Then Reina added, "We want you to understand—so you'll know—we're all in this together. Our lives we're putting into your hands."

"*Capisci*," he whispered. "I give you my word, Don, I'll respect your confidence."

Reina grinned, "We know that. We ain't fools, Charlie." He extended his hand and they shook on it all around, Reina, Lucchese, and Charlie, and then the two *tenentes* left.

Charlie was alone with Maranzano in the foyer in front of some ceramic cherubs excavated at Pompeii.

Maranzano said, "They play with each other, see, but I never learned how to play like that, Charlie. Just remember," said the don, "if you ride the carousel—be sure to ride the white horse. Now you tell me," he added, "*speak!*"

Charlie pointed out that if they were to make a deal on the terms Maranzano had just offered, there were still percentages to be worked out.

"I guarantee," the don said, clasping Charlie's shoulder, "you will be satisfied. Don Luciano. . . . Only one other small requirement," he added as Charlie later told me. The don said almost magnanimously, "Lasker and Siegel—your associates—you gotta flush them down a sewer somewhere. *Capisci*? No Jews, Charlie, on our bocce court. This is Roma, Charlie, not Jerusalem."

When Charlie left the don's estate that afternoon, he had no doubts as to what he had to do. On the ferry crossing with Genovese he fed the gulls from a bag of saltine crackers, and when each gull swept low over the wake, Charlie could hear himself whisper, "*Now*, my pet, now . . . *Now* . . . ." as, squinting, he took imaginary aim with his throwing hand at all the flocks of white and gray scavenger birds.

As he later wrote:

Lord love a duck. Man born to chaos made the son of God his island solitude. Well Bonnyrooo, but then a genie came along inside a bottle washed ashore and brought him death, like a big shiny sour apple. He could no longer be happy being simply mortal.

Likewise, with Maranzano and his ilk. We are not yet equals and when the day comes up that we are, he'll be the first to taste a lot of dirt in his mouth. I hate him and his class so low and mean . . . and greedy. Not at all the gentleman he pretends to be. Who can forgive his present wealth and status? Not Charlie Lucky. He says Death to the Calabrase because Charlie Lucky he never goes anywhere he's not wanted . . .

Chapter 7

We all met again that same evening in the rear of Marvin's Deli, an out of the way spot on Houston Street. It was certainly not the Ritz, but a lot more secure than Yonah Shlimmel's Knishe factory where you practically had to sit in the front window.

The place was closed to normal trade, as we had an interest in it for a drop, and yet the tables before us were overladen, and groaning: breads, rolls, peppers, sweet and sour tomatoes, red and green dillies, lox, cole slaw, cream cheese. There were almost as many varieties of things to eat as there are criminals in this world. Not to mention the world to come. Criminals are not united, you know; we never were.

So it was with us and, in a small way, with that deli: it served our needs, was associated with us (like Montreal used to be a Brooklyn Dodger farm team), but we didn't run it and we didn't really own it lock, stock, and herring barrels.

And sometimes that made it a lot easier to conduct business there. We could pretend to be just customers, even if and when we didn't have the appetites. The deli's actual proprietor, insofar as the Health Department was concerned, was Gurrah's brother, Fendel, a good man with the cleaver, as well as other instruments of his trade. "Eat until it kills you," he used to tell us, as a joke, "or else maybe I will."

Nevertheless that evening Fendel stayed in the back

making mushroom-barley soup as Charlie filled Ben and me in on the details of his talk with Maranzano.

"We started together, we'll finish together," Charlie told us. "No deal with Don Maranzano."

"You told that to the don?" I asked him.

Charlie tilted back in his chair and held his arms out expansively, grinning.

"What Maranzano? What don? He's an emperor—he's Julius Caesar. Mr. Goodman should make him a hat with leaves that go round the head." He made a circling gesture, like a halo, around his own head.

"I think I love you, Charlie," Ben said, gesturing grandly as he laid a plate piled high with pastrami, potato salad, cole slaw, and pickles before Charlie.

"Here's—pastrami," Ben added. "The onion—that's our engagement ring."

We all laughed and ate and ate and laughed ourselves silly. I could've kissed Charlie myself.

"You think I'd walk out on you, Benny, for a bunch of goddamn Sicilians?" Charlie teased.

Ben spoke with a mouth full of lox and bagel. He looked like a ten-year-old at his first picnic. "I don't know, Charlie. You were pretty sore at me the other night. You both were. You seemed just about ready to dump me for Vito."

"I didn't grow up with Vito," Charlie told him, pinching Ben's cheek affectionately. "Vito and me never watched out for each other. You hear me . . ."

"Look how far we've come," I told my buddies. "When I was a kid, I dreamed about being locked up all night in a delicatessen. Now we have our own keys. Fendel leaves a spread so we can talk in peace—you better take good care of him, Benny . . ."

Ben got up and crossed the counter to the cash register.

"And you know why we've come so far," I added to Charlie, my heart suddenly all aglow, "because we've got the most important key of all: we *trust* each other."

"That's better than the *dark keys* or the *white keys*, alone, on any piano," Ben added, striking the register so that the bell rang, as if to punctuate my statement. Then he stuffed a hundred-dollar bill into Fendel's drawer. "That's what we got going, all right," Ben said. "Trust. . . . like the banks."

"What about the banks?" Charlie seemed a bit confused.

I explained, "If the Irish still went to Irish banks, Italians to Italian banks, Jews to Jewish banks, the banking business'd still be like a delicatessen. They learned a new way in America. So did we. We're the melting pot personified, Charlie. All the gristle and bone stuff goes into the same cauldron and out of it you get a piece of good shortening."

I got up and pulled my briefcase out from under the table, bringing a clean table over next to ours. "And that's why we're going to win!" I added, dumping the contents of my briefcase on the table. "I got the tapes, a fortune here, some ledgers. You want to go over the day?"

Charlie looked at the bundles of cash and checks and shook his head.

"Not tonight. Tonight I'm going to show you how successful we *really* are. After this we're all going out and get us some ice cream."

I packed up the day's business and we left to walk around the corner. Ben walked with his arm around Charlie's shoulder and Charlie rested his hand on mine, like they tell me the Italian men still do in Genoa and Florence. The cool night air felt great and we were all in fine spirits. It felt good to be alive in the company of my pals. We stopped in front of the only store on the dark narrow street. "Hand Made Italian Ices and Ice Cream" glowed in red and green neon.

"Mr. Luciano!" the proprietor greeted Charlie, a big round man with drooping eyelids who chewed on the stubble of a burnt-out cigar that hung from his thick moist lips.

"What'll it be?" he said, wiping his hands on a clean white butcher's apron folded over across his ice-cream belly. "The usual?"

"You make the best hot fudge in all New York," Charlie told him, "and you could also teach Dolly Madison a thing or two about vanilla ice cream. Sure, the usual."

"Make that two," Ben and me spoke at the same time and we all laughed again. I dug into my hot fudge, and all of a sudden I started feeling anxious about Charlie and Maranzano. If this guy thinks he's Julius Caesar, I said to myself, how's he going to let Charlie off the hook so easy. Emperors don't like "no"—it doesn't fit the image. I wanted to talk some to Charlie, but I didn't trust that ice-cream vendor, Provolare, and wasn't sure how to begin.

"Listen, Charlie, I want to talk some more about this deal that fell through," I told him.

Charlie looked at his watch as he spooned the last bit of gooey fudge from his plate.

"Not now, Michael," Charlie stood up. "Tomorrow we'll talk some more. It's late. I gotta get going. You keep Benny, the slow eater here, company, while he finishes up. I'll see you in the morning."

"All right," I told him. But I wasn't happy. I don't know. Something made me edgy. I couldn't really put my finger on it.

Chapter **8**

Isn't it odd the way you sometimes have a second sense something will happen. Not *déjà vu*; quite the opposite—a sort of forward look across the abyss. I couldn't say what I knew, or how. I just knew that—no good was coming at us right away.

When Charlie left Ben and me at the ice-cream stand, he passed a drunk down the dark street in front of his car.

162

The guy panhandled Charlie for the price of a cup of coffee and being generous-hearted, Charlie said, "Will five bucks do?"

He reached into his pocket for some cash at which moment the rummy had found a sap he'd hidden in his sleeve and gave Charlie a backhanded bop across the temple—had him seeing nothing but acres of soft black velvet.

A big black Hudson rolled by just then and its back door swung open as it braked. The drunk and a guy from the front seat next to the driver stowed Charlie's unconscious body inside, like a duffel bag being shipped off to camp. No doubt somebody else somewhere else was already mixing up a batch of cement for Charlie's ultimate resting place. The drunk went staggering down those dark streets toward the Staten Island ferry.

It didn't take Ben and me very long to figure Charlie had been kidnapped. He was usually as punctual as clockwork and he'd told us he was going to meet Joy at the Waldorf at 11 P.M. I had to talk to him about something and when he didn't get there after an hour or so, I went back to that dark street and there was a fresh pack of Charlie's Sweet Caporals. It must have fallen from his pocket into the gutter. I rushed right over to the Waldorf to call Ben and keep Joy company.

Let me just tell you, I was in a rage, a regular tumult. We just don't do things this way, *ever*, if we can avoid it. The Italian Mustache Petes, back then, did, though, because they didn't know any better. I think such ignorance they had and callous brutality. Nothing worse in the whole world. I saw the *Godfather*—parts One and Two—and there they speak of codes of honor and respect and whatnot, but let me tell you something. As Professor Hobsbaum, a Britisher, has put it so aptly, "The poor of Naples tend to idealize gangsters in a way vaguely reminiscent of social banditry" and there's just "no evidence" that they "have ever deserved any such idealization whatsoever."

When it happens, they go after your best friend in the whole wide world, you can sometimes get that way especially if you got any *sechel*, whatsoever. So I was telling all this to poor Joy in the Waldorf that night just to keep our minds off of all our troubles and worries and grief while Ben and his boys scoured the city for Charlie, and I'm afraid I must have sounded a little dry because she interrupted me right then.

"*Jews . . . gentiles . . .* what difference?" she said. 'A butcher is a butcher and you're in the butcher-shop business."

"Easy, Joy," I said. "We'll find him."

I didn't know whether to believe my own words. Rigid with shock and fear, she sat on the big Art Deco loveseat, below the Erte paintings of circus freaks, fighting to control her fears. She could hardly control her speech so that it was coherent. The lacquered nails of one hand were digging so deep and hard into the meaty part of the other that they drew a little blood.

Joy was trying hard not to break down. She spoke out of the side of her mouth, but you heard a suppressed sob and a gasp with every word.

"I'd rather be his mistress than his wife, I always said, Michael. We had a meal together, about two o'clock, just like man and wife. Then he said he was meeting you guys and had another meeting afterward. You know me, I thought he meant Capone's bitch, Chris. But it's not her; I know it because I checked. She's just as upset as me. I acted to her just like a wife, Michael: not so much irate as concerned. But I'm glad now we're not married because if we ever were . . . I'd feel . . . I'd feel . . ."

Her voice trembled in her, forcing a shudder through her shoulders.

I sat there, grim-faced by her side, listening to her, watching her nails knife into her palm, and then I reached out and broke the grip one hand was forcing down against the other.

"Joy," I said. "Please be good to yourself."

"Find him, Mike. Please?" She begged me. "Find him."

I told her Benny had everybody out in the streets, Vito's

bunch, Lepke's, even the police, and Fendel with his cleaver.

She went over to the bar and took a cut-crystal decanter and poured some liquor out into a glass.

Her hands were shaking so badly she dribbled some of the liquor on her silk wrapper. "I'm all right. See. I'm doing fine."

She tried to smile, and the effect was grotesque, as if the ripeness seizing her and flushing out her cheeks was simply all. "Did you call Polly Adler's? Chris might have been selling me a bill of goods."

"No bill," I said, "no goods. We found his car and a full packet of Caporals. He never even left Spring Street."

Joy said, "He had a gun. He always has a gun. He'll be all right with his gun on him, won't he?"

The assurances from me her eyes were pleading for I could not, with true candor, give Joy now. I truly thought the worst had happened. They'd find his body behind a bush somewhere.

Joy's thinking must've paralleled my own. Abruptly her voice turned shrill. "Damn you!" She threw the glass at my face, and it crashed behind me against the wall. I felt the splash, and a fragment of glass against my cheek as I took the hit, and Joy's angry words, "Damn every one of you."

My cheek was bleeding spirits mixed with blood. I wiped it with a hanky and got up to go to the phone. 'I'll call Ruth. She'll stay with you. We love you, Joy . . . . . You must know that . . . any way it turns out."

And that was true, too. I figured if the worst happened, I would be sure she got a handsome annuity for life, and the same for Charlie's parents, and any other next of kin. Chrissy I felt different about. If she was in on this scam in any way through that capon Capone, I'd have to cut her dead. Even so I regarded her as the mistress, more than the wife, and since there was no will from Charlie saying otherwise, I would give to her only on a need-to-know basis. Let her hock some of her damn rocks, and other things. I would say our books were open for everybody to see, but what was Charlie's was going to Mr. and Mrs. L, and to Joy.

In fact, Charlie was not yet dead. He wasn't even pro-bated. He'd been taken to a warehouse off Baltic Avenue in the Greenpoint section of Brooklyn and slashed and beaten, kicked, and schlammed unmercifully from pillar to post by these three thugs in Masseria, or Maranzano's, employment; we weren't sure then which it was.

He lay beneath one bare bulb on a hard concrete floor in a puddle of his own fluids. And with his ankles trussed and his hands tied behind his back, they were still going at him.

It must have been painful to remember and damn near impossible to forget: so much brutalization and torture. One of them now held a knife to his throat, as if about to butcher a kid, an only kid, or perhaps the sacrificial suckling pig.

"Feeling better, Charlie?" He couldn't rise and yet he struggled to, and when he did, a fist from somewhere sent him crashing back again.

Again Charlie tried to rise and couldn't; on all fours he crawled away from his tormentors, a mutilated animal.

"He stinks on ice," one of them said. "Luciano even makes the ice stink, if you ask me, he stinks so much."

"Na, he's okay," said another. "He can even crawl."

"Show us, Charlie. Show us how nice you crawl." They tormented their victim, Mr. Charlie Luciano.

Inch by inch, blood blinding his sight, Charlie told me he had crawled across the cement.

The first thug spoke like the straight man in a comedy routine. "Where's he crawling?"

"He's crawling to see Suzie," the other answered.

"Who's Suzie?"

"If you knew Suzie, Like I knew Suzie, oh, oh, oh, What a girl."

Just like the comedian Eddie Cantor sang such lines, punctuating each "oh" with a kick against Charlie's broken body.

The straight man leaned over and spoke to Charlie in a

mock-earnest voice of reminder, of something or other. "Charlie—it's all finished now. You can go home."

Charlie struggled to gain his knees and crawl, when the other thug kicked him again in the groin. "When in doubt," he said, winking at his partner, "punt and he'll *pass* out."

"Honestly, Charlie," the other started up again. "All finished. No kidding. Good night, Charlie."

Clawing himself once more to his hands and knees, Charlie groped and struggled forward until he encountered a third pair of legs. Then the thug bent over and pulled Charlie to his feet.

"Charlie—you hear me, *Charlie*?" Charlie heard nothing, so the last guy took a bottle of smelling salts from his pocket and waved it under that mashed mess of broken bone which was sort of dangling off Charlie's face.

"We got a message for you from somebody you know who wanted to be a friend," he added as Charlie came to, his head bobbing up, as if on a thread.

"When Julius Caesar, when he used to take a prisoner— even a king, a big king like you—Caesar brought him home in a cage."

He heaved Charlie backward into the arms of the others who threw him crashing to the floor.

"See how lucky you are, Charlie?" The man who played straight man smiled at Charlie. "No cage for *you*. Only us," he added, taking another knife from his pocket. The shiny steel blade glared under the light.

"We've been fooling with you, Charlie," he said through his frozen smile. "Now we're going to get very serious. Now we get sincere." The smile disintegrated, his lips tightened and twitched into meanness, his eyes squeezing into slits as he cut.

Chapter 9

When the phone rang, Ben and I both lunged toward it at the same time.

"Hello," Ben said.

"Benny?" It was Hearn. "You better get out to Hylan Boulevard on Staten Island. They just found Charlie. . . . I don't know—they think he's dead. I'm sorry, Ben."

I was glad I had Ruthie to stay with Joy, and the doctor had given her something to make her sleep.

When we got to Hylan Boulevard, Charlie was being rolled toward the ambulance on a gurney.

"Is he alive?" I asked the cop who was blocking my way to Charlie.

"Just keep going, buddy," he told me.

"My name's Lasker."

"Yes, sir. Well, sir, sort of." He shined his flashlight toward the head of the gurney. Charlie's face was barely recognizable: steak tartar.

"He's still bleeding," Ben said, touching Charlie's cheek.

"As long as he's bleeding," I said, "he's alive. Bleed, Charlie," I added. "Just a little bit longer, pal."

"Before this one's over," Ben said, "the whole world's going to be bleeding."

The next day at the hospital Charlie had a lot of visitors. His face was completely bandaged, and the tubes were going in and out of him like Grand Central Station. He breathed, heavily, under an oxygen tent, and I never heard a sweeter sound than that slow persistent breathing of my oldest friend.

Mrs. Luciano leaned close over the transparent plastic oxygen tent covering him.

"Poppa's sick. He's sick, or he come to see you. He loves you, Sallie. You know he loves you? All the presents you send. He keep them now. He know they come from your heart. You rest, Sallie. I sit by the bed. Sleep, my son, my Sallie."

Mrs. Luciano clutched a handkerchief in her fist and dabbed at her eyes, every so often, while she stared straight ahead into the gauze mask that had become Charlie's face.

We didn't know if he could hear us or not. It didn't seem to matter, just then. He was alive, and everyone had to talk to him, had to treat him like he *had* heard and knew we were there, just rooting for him.

"They say you're going to do fine, Charlie," Ben told him. "Hardly a mark. You know what they're calling you out there? Lucky Luciano. Charlie Luck himself."

Ben started out cheerful, but his voice soon broke, and in a throaty croak he pleaded, "Who did it, Charlie? Who did it to you?" When he got no answer, Ben reassured Charlie as if he had.

"Don't worry, Charlie. Sooner or later . . . sooner or later."

I had to talk to Charlie too.

"Out there, they're killing each other pretty good, Charlie. Maybe a couple of hundred already dead. That's some war. Nobody touches you here. You got more guards than the President."

Over the next couple of days I tried to get Charlie to talk and tell me who was responsible for what had happened to him. Later he told us all he could remember from that time was a series of dreams, like his life flashing before his eyes. The things he thought he had forgotten and then later he also came up with the various images, too, of cruelty and pain, that bare bulb, the warehouse floor, his shame.

169

He even went all the way back to his childhood to the day Valenti came knocking on Mr. Goodman's door while Charlie was sitting on the rocker in the back room, playing with Sheba, the kitten.

"It was so real, Michael," Charlie said. "Valenti's face—the face of death—was pressing against Mr. Goodman's door. And the sound of his ring, rapping against the glass. It was all so clear like it was happening to me only yesterday."

Charlie was getting very excited. The gauze over his face was now suffused with a clotted brownish serum. I wasn't so sure this was good for him, so I tried to change the subject.

"You don't remember your visitors? Remember Joy? And Chris?"

Joy had come to the hospital when Charlie was still out of it, and she had spoken to him, like the rest of us . . . quietly . . . and just so glad he was alive.

"I'm glad we're just part time, Charlie," she had teased him lovingly. "Otherwise I might be feeling bad. You wouldn't want me to feel bad, would you?" The tears streamed down her cheeks. She wiped them and took a deep breath. Sounding cheerful, she told Charlie, "P. S. I love you. But don't take it seriously."

Charlie later didn't remember a thing of Joy's visit.

Chris too had come to the hospital and tried to get Charlie to talk and tell her who had done this to him.

"I called Chicago, Charlie. I was talking with Mr. Capone and when I told him, you know he just laughed. He said somebody had saved him the trouble. I don't know—the way he said it—maybe it was Capone who did it. Do you think it could have been one of Al's people?"

Chris didn't have any more luck than the rest of us when she gave him her own private message, "We never gave ourselves a chance, did we, Charlie? I spoiled it all a long time ago. But I'll do anything. *Anything* you ask me to," she added. 'Only live, Charlie, don't please die."

It was strange. Charlie had seemed uninterested in hearing what his visitors had said when he was unconscious. All he felt like doing was telling me his dreams. It was weird, the way he didn't want to talk about anything else. Maybe he was on the edge, between life and death, when he was dreaming. I just don't know.

"Mr. Goodman came to me, Michael, and you know what he said? He spoke to me, but what he said were the identical words Joe Masseria had told me at the meeting in the brownstone. 'What do you think, Charlie? Everybody dances and you sit by the wall and watch? The music plays.'" And then Charlie made the sound of a machine gun—baabbaabbaabaa. "'Everybody dances. Nobody sits.'"

The nurse walked in then and told Charlie he had to rest.

"In a little while," he said.

Then he continued. "I dreamed my father came to visit me, that time I was in prison. You know I really wanted him to come, but he never did. In my dream he came, and I was running, like in slow motion, to get to him, and when I finally saw him, it was a replay of the time the feds came to the house to put me in the can, and my father slapped me, called me 'Bum!' I had to stop him from hitting me again; I grabbed his wrist, forced his hand to my lips and kissed it, like he was my personal pontiff."

I interrupted. "I love you, Charlie Lucky. Please just live."

"And I was crying. Just bawling," Charlie went on. "*Me ken meharget verin*," he added in Yiddish. "It was such a disappointment to me. I was crying, and then I came to. I came out of it, and I swear, Michael, I felt tears, the salt stinging my cheeks under the bandages, and that's what brought me out when I did."

Chapter 10

Years later I heard from Ruthie how Chris and Joy finally met in the hospital cafeteria, after visiting Charlie, over bowls of green Jell-o salad with pot cheese and chopped apples mélanged with raisins. Rice pudding too, I think.

These two stunning babes were at opposite tables spooning their stuff into their made-up mouths and faces, like beautiful people in a moving picture, when they noticed each other, and each knew immediately who the other was, and there they just were. No sense in any more of this pretended silence and disinterest. After each eyeing the other, with the searching respect of tigresses, there commenced, as we say, the following conversation:

Joy to Chris: "You're very beautiful."

"So are you," Chris said. "And that does not surprise me. Does Charlie ever talk about me?" Chris asked.

"A little."

"I've heard a lot about you," Chris said. "You're his favorite blonde."

"For a while." Joy looked a little downcast.

Chris asked, "Want to swap?"

"Thanks," Joy shook her head. "I'll take what I've got."

"I do what I can for him," Chris said. "I take chances—to tell him the things he has to know. I don't think you could do that."

"If you mean the chances," Joy said, "you're probably right. I couldn't. Charlie never complained about the way I made love, however."

"Is that why he's always been so loyal to you?"

"I sleep with him," Joy said. "And I will again, if and when he gets better."

"And so will I," Chris said, accepting the distinction Joy was making, "from time to time."

"And so you will, I'm sure," said Joy.

They went upstairs to see Charlie together, which was maybe the second reason people called him Charlie Lucky! A man would be fortunate enough to have just one of those women on a string; two were simply aces, as we say. But Charlie had others, too, when he eventually recuperated. The two women became close and helped to guard his hand which was a sort of royal flush.

When Charlie finally left the hospital, he looked like a different man; there was so much scar tissue on his face. Ben called for Charlie at the hospital and brought him home, under an armed guard. He opened the door to Charlie's suite where I was sitting with the books and drew the drapes open for Charlie so the light flooded the room.

A table full of delicatessen had been set out on the buffet, and Charlie's fingers speared a pickled tomato. As he sucked off the sour bitter juice from it, his fingers went up to his face and touched those many new scars striating it.

He went over to the mirror then to look at himself. Anxious to distract him, I emerged from the shadows of an alcove with our ledgers.

"While you were getting better, Charlie, we were getting better—a lot better. Take a look."

I gave him the open ledger where there was just a column of figures referring to our receipts from vending machines, a new sideline: three and a half million dollars and growing on an investment of less than one hundred thousand dollars.

Charlie didn't seem that interested, or appreciative.

"Thanks, Michael," he said as he placed the ledgers back in my hands. He wandered over toward an easy chair and sat down.

Ben tried to show off our caterer's table once more. This wasn't the work of Fendel; it was a Ruben's cornucopia

173

holiday special. The tongues had tongues, the salamis little salamis.

Ben asked, "How do you like all this? What I brought you here. It's the whole delicatessen. A lot better than that hospital food."

He grabbed up one of the plates. "What do you want, Charlie? I'll fix up a plate for you."

"I want to talk," Charlie said.

Ben and I looked at each other like we'd just fixed a CCNY basketball game together. He left the half-filled plate on the sofa and said, "So we'll talk."

I sat down next to Charlie and he said, "There were five men that night: the one who sapped me on the street and the four who did the job."

Ben said, "So we'll find them."

"I don't *have* to find them," Charlie said, "because I know who paid them."

Next to him on a lamp table was a silver humidor. A silver cup of wooden matches had tumbled over by its side. Charlie reached for a match and turned it over and over in his hands.

Ben asked, "Who paid them?"

Charlie explained, as if he were talking to kids, "He didn't want to kill me. If he wanted me dead, I would be dead. He was giving me a little lesson. And now *I'm* going to do a little teaching, too."

"Who was it?" Ben asked. "Tell us? *Who?*"

"Hail Caesar," went Charlie. He snapped the match stick. "*Caesarum ave rex fongo la mamma!*"

We were all silent, more or less flabbergasted, and immobilized too by Charlie's erudite display of Latin and Sicilian.

"Oh," Ben finally said.

He turned to scoop up his coat and moved toward the door.

"Benny." Charlie was giving orders and Ben hesitated.

"He'll be dead before dark," Ben assured us.

Charlie said, "*You'll* be dead before dark." He flung the

174

broken match aside. "If I wanted a torpedo, I'd have told you in the hospital. His house, his offices, it's all fortresses. His women and children live behind a castle keep. He has ears on his ears, eyes for his eyes, and a temper such as you wouldn't want to have hit you. Ever . . .

"You can't reach him," Charlie said. "Forget it. Nobody can reach him by the normal means . . . except Joe the Boss . . ."

Ben stayed leaning against the door jamb. "Masseria?" he repeated.

And I said, "You're going to enter the war?"

Charlie regarded us bleakly. The new scar tissue on his face gleamed against his otherwise sallow complexion. "Where the hell do you two think I've been?"

I nodded. "So you'll join Masseria."

"*Miseria mia*," went Ben.

I reminded Charlie, "Masseria tried to kill *me*, Charlie."

With that same vast air of bleakness, he said, "I've got troubles of my own."

He grabbed the big ledger book from the table by his side. "Our books are closed from now on, Benny, Michael. They're closed until I open them again."

He threw the ledger at my feet. "You've got no part in this, Mickey. I don't want to see you two again until I'm ready. Go. Take a trip—you've been talking about a new alcohol supply from the Caribbean. Well, go see what it looks like."

He shifted his scarred gaze toward Ben. "You, when I need, I'll call. Meantime don't take any wooden chippies."

Hurt for a moment, Ben replied, "You need me now, you know you do, Charlie."

Luciano stood and his tiredness and the heaviness on his lips and body seemed almost tangible.

"I've lately lost all my mirth. Indeed it goes so ill with me I need just to rest awhile. If you two ever loved me, forget fooling around right now. I'll be off, and later there's only one more thing I want from either of you . . ."

He left us alone to go into his bedroom. Ben and I were

hurt and puzzled, confused. Not even to touch a piece of pastrami. To be so withdrawn and secretive in his rage for revenge.

Ben said, "How can we stop him?"

"Stop him?" I said, fearing the worst between us would happen, was in fact happening already. "It's over, Benny."

I picked up the ledger with its heavy reckoning of all our various accounts together and dropped it with a thump across the table.

Chapter 11

Charlie's father never lived to see his son's revenge. A few days after Charlie's release from the hospital he dropped dead of an aneurysm. He had instructed the Workmen's Circle to turn over the few hundred dollars in savings he had carefully hoarded for a future grandson and left behind a note for his son's edification as well:

Dear Son,
    You read this after I die. There is no heaven and no hell.
    Don't listen to the priests and the politicians. They only wish to live good.
    You good boy.
    Take good care of your momma.
    Viva Garibaldi!
    Live Charlie. Your father he loves you and he always loved you.

It really got to Charlie, I think, this message from the grave. In the days following the hasty funeral at Little Sons of Italy and the interment in Rocky Point, Long Island, Charlie went back twice to the grave with flowers, to talk to his old man's spirit, hovering in the ether above.

"I'm sorry I never made you proud of me, Poppa," was his message over and over again, as if he had entirely dispelled the portent of that old man's dying testament.

The last time he went, Ben and I went along in the limousine and afterward we drove back to Wyandanch on Long Island to a building construction site. The place was vast, vacant, and dusty, with little low stakes of wood pounded into the raw earth and attached by thin strings.

It was getting close to twilight. There were three big Hudsons parked, or rather stationed at the perimeters of the vast area, and a fourth up to its hubcaps in dust and raw earth in the center.

From every angle Pete Morello, who was now Masseria's chief bodyguard, had posted guards, and when we three drove up, Morello came out from behind the cover of his car and opened the door for us.

He walked with us as escort to that enormous custom Hudson in the center where Joe the Boss, bloated and sleek, had regally ensconced himself.

When Charlie and Masseria came eye-to-eye and face-to-face, their eyes held for a moment as Luciano spoke. "You once said the next time we met we'd be friends or enemies."

"*Si!*"

Masseria extended his hand, an offering of sorts, and Charlie seemed to kneel a little as he bent to kiss it.

Such obsequiousness turned our stomachs, Ben's especially, so I started up the car then and drove off into the dust but not until I saw Charlie and Masseria enthroned in the back seat of the big Hudson and all the other gunsels and schlammers moving off rapidly to their other cars.

After that, things began to happen in our industry in quick succession. Reina was murdered in cold blood, and Tommy Lucchese almost got hit, too, except he was warned by our man Genovese. Joe the Boss now knew all and his wrath was bloody revenge.

The things men do to each other when they are angry for some reason . . .

As Genovese once put it to me, "You think Masseria lived this long because he's as stupid as he looks?"

Reina got blown with a shotgun from ten feet away as he was about to enter The Pomadero, a steak restaurant in Bay Ridge.

Molo Cantori, another turncoat, got hit with a pickaxe from behind on his skull one evening as he was coming out of a prize fight at Sunnyside Gardens.

China Dragon was burned, and Macho Negro, the Cuban snow dealer, was passed through a sewer filter, with his eyes open.

The center of that whole killing operation was still Masseria's old bottling plant in the produce center, a well-fortified headquarters. Morello's soldiers were posted everywhere throughout that part of Little Italy, as if guarding some bivouac encampment; at night he had them sleep on mattresses on the floor. The so-called Sicilian vespers, then, was just another squalid war for revenge, among other things.

Once Charlie and Masseria held a powwow there, with only Morello present. Ostensibly they were just going over the books, but it turned out, as usual, their main book was revenge.

Rage—rage—rage—such rage we had for each other in those days. No wonder all the little people on the streets were afraid of us.

During even the worst of times Masseria's bottling operation continued. That day, though, everybody had been dismissed, aside from a couple of co-workers and Morello's Praetorian Guard.

It was Morello's privilege to enter Masseria's makeshift office at the bottling plant without knocking. The Boss of Bosses ignored him and continued to peel an apple, the long spiral of that skin unbroken by his expert shiv work with the knife. Masseria listened while Charlie summarized his economic strategy for this new gangland war.

178

"You see these figures here," Charlie said, pointing to a sheet of paper he held before the Boss, "that's what Maranzano's taking out of Chicago—the last two weeks from Joe Aiello. Here," he added, pointing to another column, "is what he took last month—and here, the month before."

Charlie tossed the computations on Masseria's desk while the fat man sliced and quartered his apple, his cheeks bulging with the tart pulpy fruit.

"You want to reach Maranzano," Charlie continued, "cut off his money. Cut off Aiello. We'll do the work. We'll need Capone's permission."

Masseria seemed pleased. He stretched out his arms over his desk like the pope delivering a benediction and said, "Go—talk to him—take care of it."

On his way out, Charlie stopped and turned at the doorway, "One more thing. Killing Reina was a big mistake."

Charlie always had guts. No one ever dared tell Masseria he had made a boo-boo, *or* a wrong move. The Boss pouted and licked his knife, frustrated by the pith of Charlie's words and the fact that he was still starved after devouring his apple.

"Charlie, killing Reina was a mistake like Christ walking on the water," he said. "People expect too much from me now. *So.* If I didn't?" he asked. "*What then*? Sure, I let him betray me," he said sarcastically. "You like that better?"

"You were too greedy, Joe. You wanted too much. For a few thousand bucks you could've turned him around—let him go to Maranzano. You could've had your own spy right in the middle of his big camp."

Masseria scowled a few seconds, then opened the drawer of his desk and withdrew a big red Gross Michel Haitian banana from his five-pound stash. He couldn't bear to have more than one of his many appetites denied him at once. He grinned, as his mood suddenly shifted, and he peeled the banana.

"*See*?" He spoke to Morello. "That's why *Charlie* here is with us." Masseria tapped his temple with his banana. "Smart. Brains like a Jew. And Italian courage. You listen to him—you do what he says." Morello's face registered nothing. He nodded stoically at his boss.

"This Chicago business. I want Joe Adonis and Albert Anastasia. They'll work with Vito." Charlie presented his plan.

"You're the boss, Charlie," Masseria said. "Give him what he needs," he told Morello as he left the office with Charlie.

The two men headed toward the gunmen sleeping in their clothes at the bottom of the stairway. "Adonis. Anastasia. Front and center!" Like they were drill sergeants rousing the troops.

"Let's go, Adonis. Come on, handsome!" Morello woke the sleeping beauties, then shook still another by his side. "Pick up your socks!" Morello barked. "Albert? Anastasia? Kiss your mattress good-bye. You're going to Chicago."

Chapter 12

Charlie took a late night flight to Chicago with Adonis and Anastasia. He didn't want to spend any more time in Chicago than was necessary. He called Capone from the Midway Airport. Capone's voice was husky and welcoming.

"We end up on the same side—Capone and Luciano—so I tell you something, Charlie, you got guts and brains."

"And scars," Charlie added to remind Scarface Capone of what had been done to him.

They made a date for early the next morning.

Capone was still in his pajamas—white silk with "A. C."

monogrammed in black on the pocket—when Charlie entered his lavish hotel suite at the Drake.

Charlie sat in a striped velvet wing-back chair, almost blinded by all the glitter. One wall was papered with gold lamé, another was plastered with floor-to-ceiling mirrors. A huge crystal and cut-glass chandelier hung above a fountain: Venus on the half shell—a large naked marble lady with long tresses who stood on a marble clam shell while the water spurted all around.

Capone ate breakfast, lifting silver plate covers from a large glass cart that had been wheeled in a moment before. "I feel sick—what they done to you in New York, Charlie. Like animals."

"Sure, Al, I know how hard you took it. Now we're talking about Joe Aiello."

"I don't need no imported guns," Capone told him.

"That's why he's still walking around. How many times have you already tried to kill him?"

Capone got mad and broke a slice of toast he was buttering. He smiled and took another slice.

"He's like Joe the Boss. He dances through the rain; he don't get wet so easy."

Capone rose from his breakfast and crossed the room toward a low square table covered with green velvet that draped to the floor. He lifted the cloth and a safe was revealed underneath. Covering the lock with his body, he clicked the combination open and pored through a pile of newspaper clippings and photographs he drew out from the top shelf.

On the floor in the hallway leading toward the bedroom, Charlie also noticed a pretty pair of gold sequined high-heeled sandals.

"Joe Aiello," Capone said, handing him a picture cut out from a newspaper.

Charlie studied the grainy photo, the long thin face and pointed bird nose under the fedora brim before him.

"You better be right," he told Capone flatly.

Exasperated, Capone threw his hands up. "Maybe I made

181

a mistake. I got him confused with my dentist," he said. "Har har har." He looked at Charlie as if to warn him. "That's twice now, Luciano, you question my judgment. One more time—the Sicilians, they say three is a magic number."

Charlie rose from his chair and turned abruptly when the bedroom door opened.

Wearing a long black negligee with a deep V cut out down the front and the back, Chris Brennan sauntered forth.

Capone helped himself to another piece of dry toast from the breakfast tray while Charlie and Chris stared at each other, startled and a little embarrassed.

"Chris Brennan." Capone made the introductions. "You met her at Maranzano's place. Charlie Luciano."

"I don't believe I've had the pleasure recently," Charlie smirked. "But I remember you, of course. How are you, Miss Brennan?" She was fresh from bed and her face had that soft hazy look of a woman just awakened from a pleasant dream, of one sort or another.

"Just fine, Mr. Luciano." She smiled at him, and Charlie felt his groin tighten. Tearing his eyes from hers, he glanced down at the clipping in his hand once more.

"Won't you have a cup of coffee?" she asked Charlie.

"No, thanks, I must be moving on. Business." He folded the clipping and placed it in his breast pocket.

"Be in touch," he told Capone on his way out the door. "Some other time, Miss Brennan."

Chapter 13

It was beefsteak tartar finally for Aiello, also. He got it later that same month of pogroms, from a pair of Thompsons fired at close range by Joe Adonis and Albert Anastasia in front of Aiello's West Chicago apartment building.

Genovese was there as point man, and he told me they had to scrape what was left of Aiello's bodyguard, Biancoli Borge, off the sidewalks with a pair of flexible steel snow shovels.

The reason I didn't hear about it until after it happened was that I'd gone to Havana at the time, looking for new suppliers. And what a place that was in those days—wide open, with every attraction, too: balmy breezes, sun, and beach, maraca and marimba bands, even gambling. The most beautiful women I've ever seen anywhere. Best dressed, too. Even the hookers. And for money people did anything for you.

Gave you a show, that is. That wasn't the only thing. There was Poppa Bouchard's, where the most beautiful female impersonators I ever saw cavorted in the latest Paris fashions.

Shortly after I checked into the old National Hotel in Havana, I sent Ruthie a postcard:

What a place this is. Regular Coney Island in the Tropics. Lido Beach with palm trees: beautiful people, colorful diseases, exotic poverty. Enough cruelty to satisfy even Al

Capone. Whomever. The girls are pretty, but none like you.
Stay sweet. Love M

To Charlie I also dropped a line or two:

Rum and Coca Cola Charlie there oughta be a song. This
whole place could be had for a song. Cuba Libre: our whole
business and this place were made for each other like peas
and rice, or ham and melon. Everybody's on the take here.
You have to bribe the police to let you cross the streets.
Nice little town to do business in.

I also wrote Momma in the mountains where she was
for the holidays:

Kosher it's not, but warm it is. Your son is having a won-
derful time in the sunny tropics. You should see what people
eat here, pig tails, and all sorts of roots I never saw anywhere else. Today I had a milk shake made with a banana
and something else called *guanabana*, a little like a bland
sort of nectarine. They say it's good for the runs. For what
ails you. Your son Michael.

Later that same night I wrote Ruthie again:

Did you know Cuba has its own baseball teams? Department
stores? They call it the Pearl of the Antilles . . . Your diamond in the rough, Michael.

There were all those palacios along the Miramar, the
lush countryside. There were streets teeming with poverty—
urchins everywhere, rum, disease, and all that moist, fecund
heat of midday.

The only place worse I ever saw was Managua, Nicaragua, under the first Somoza. There they actually had
places you could eat human flesh, in a coriander sauce, if
you fancied it.

But in Havana the old Adam ruled in a world that had
lost all innocence. Every child was a beggar. They dueled

for pennies with pet scorpions, sold you their sisters, their mothers, their child-bride wives. And such depravity. You name it. The tropics have a very special allure for degenerates, I think.

I wrote Ruthie another card:

Tell your dad the men still wear celluloid collars to work, and it's 100 degrees in the shade. All kinds all colors here: regular potpourri. You even hear a little Yiddish, but everybody has such a dark skin who can tell? I bought you a fan, and a basket made out of bulrushes, and for Momma a black mantilla such as the real old *yentas* wear. Be good to yourself, my love. Soon, M.

In a second postal card to Charlie I further declared:

Anything you want for yourself or Ben tell me—a fancy Panama hat, or suede shoes. Just send me cutouts, or a pattern with your size air mail.

Charlie was much too busy to write back.

But when I called long distance to arrange to have some of our funds transferred from a bank in Miami, Charlie told me Joy had been to see Ruthie yesterday and it could happen any day now; I was going to be a father.

Then I called Ruthie and all she said was, "I'm all right but hurry home, Michael. Please. I can feel the heart beating. *Hurry*."

Even in Cuba, however, I was strictly business. I'm having this conversation one day with Bacardi, a big man in cane sugar. And I ask him how he could let people live like this? In their own filth? And disease?

"O señor," he says with a shrug, "if it were in my power to do anything about it, but it's not, you see . . . we are all just as helpless as they."

I fell in love with the place at first glance. This Cuba. Eventually it became an obsession with me. Then it was mostly a new dealer's outlet for buying cane alcohol, ninety to one hundred percent pure: rum, and what they called overproof, one hundred ninety proof in other words. And molasses as well.

We were loading the stuff one day from some ancient white trucks, just like we used to use, into the beaten-up coastal steamer, and as the drums rolled aboard, all the kids of Havana were calling out, begging for *"plata," "dinero," "un duro señor, por favor!"* etcetera, etcetera, etcetera. The Cuban foreman, Rigoberto Lopez Perez, oiled with his own sweat, called out to me: *"Hola!"* I walked over to where he was directing a sweating crew of black men to unload big twenty-gallon drums of molasses.

The foreman was a white man, with yellowish skin, bulging pectorals, crinkly black hair in waves and kinks all over his pomaded head, the obvious signs of earlier generations of deliberate racial confusion. I had been told by Longey's people in Newark to keep a sharp eye out for bimbos like him because they had been known to do a certain amount of skimming, and adulterating, for that matter.

But it wasn't that way at all with Lopez Perez, or Rigoberto, as I preferred to call him. He was honest as a bright Caribbean morning and opened the lids of every drum for me to inspect just to assure me I was getting my money's worth.

When we shared some of my Lucky Strikes afterward, he said, "Señor Lasker, have you ever heard or read of José Marti?"

"Was he some kind of baseball player?" I asked.

"Beisbol? No señor," he said. "José Marti was our greatest poet, and *periodista—journalista*, and a teacher, too. He drove out the Spanish, and was Cuba's greatest patriot, and when he lived in your New York in exile, he was treated just like a . . . *speak*," he added.

"Speak?"

"Speak," he said strongly, "is not a nice word. The gringos use it too much. If you are not one of them, you

could also be a friend of Cuba. We sure need friends. We Cubans."

His face gleamed, a splendid sweating brow. I didn't want to get messed up with politics. What did I know about that sort of thing? I decided to make a joke of it: "Any friend of Cuba's, Rigoberto I assure you is a friend of mine."

"Señor Lasker," he shook his head at me sadly. "I am not a funny person, so don't laugh at me please."

Later that same day in a waterfront cantina I was drinking cold fresh-squeezed orange juice, which they used to make down there like no place in the world, including Collins Avenue, Miami Beach, when two rough characters in ragged, sweat-stained tropical suits entered and came right over to my table.

One was muscular, with a fierce Carib Indian face, and tribal markings; the other seemed suave by comparison, a dark-skinned man with dead black eyes and a look that said get out of my way, bud, or it's your funeral.

They both greeted me in Spanish, to which I replied with the customary *buenos* and then the darker one, who did most of the talking, said, "We are all Cubans . . ."

I sensed the kind of trouble toward which it is best to acknowledge right away that one will not be participating.

"There's an awful lot of Cubans here in Cuba," I nodded.

The talker agreed, with a nod back, "So, *pues*, you send our rum to the United States."

"I import *mo-lasses*," I explained.

He dismissed my distinctions with a motion of his hand. "Rum—molasses. It belongs to *us*. You pay *us*."

"I've already paid for what I've bought," I explained.

"Maybe, señor, but you didn't pay *us*," the talker said sullenly. "*Entonces* you pay *us* now."

He poked a finger toward my chest.

"Who the hell are you?" I asked.

"Me? I am the one who gives you good advice, *meester*." He turned a little toward his companion. "This

Chico here . . . he **is** the one who is going to cut your **gingo** throat *goddammit* . . . " His speech faltered; his voice trembled on him. "Excuse me, señor . . . your throat, if you know what I mean."

He **was** glancing toward the doorway **of the** café. **Under** the **blazing** black and red-gold letters of a Cienfuegos Cerveza advertisement a swarthy plump-faced man entered. He was stocky, of peasant origin, wore a white suit and a brown silk shirt open at the throat, and he did not seem to be perspiring in all that heat. He radiated such an inner calm, such a smooth dry unfurrowed brow.

Seeing him, my two *nudnick* friends seemed very troubled. They shrugged their shoulders as if to say, oh well, and started for the door.

"A misunderstanding," the talker explained. "Nothing more. Nothing less. A matter of some commerical confusion, señor . . ."

They fled out like scurrying mice.

The man in the white suit came over to my table to ask, with a grin, if they had disturbed me.

"Almost," I explained. "But I carry a little disturber of my own."

I opened my suit jacket so he could see the pearl handle of the derringer displayed in my black silk waistband.

He said, "Your name, I believe, is Lasker?"

"Michael," I said, putting it on a first-name basis.

He said, "May I sit down?"

"Por favor," I said. *"Con mucho gusto."*

"I speak English," he said. He ordered a *batido de mamey* with brown rum from the bartender, a sort of Cuban milk shake, to put it frankly, with alcohol added.

Then he put a well-manicured hand upon the table. "Those men—I assure you, señor—they will not bother you no more. They think I speak for Machado."

"Machado?"

"You don't know our esteemed Presidente Machado?"

"Never had the pleasure," I said.

He said, "The people they call him the Butcher." He

waited to see if I showed any expression. "What do such a people know anyway? They are so very poor. They have no schools to teach them nothing. Once, señor, I was mostly like them . . . I think once you were also the same."

"Lo mismo," I affirmed. "Once . . ."

He nodded. "This molasses—you buy to make the alcohol. This is for yourself?"

"Only for myself."

"Then you are two people," he corrected me. "I read the *Miami Herald* and *Time* magazine. You are the partner, they say there, of Charlie Lucky . . . Luciano . . . a powerful man."

"I buy for myself," I insisted. "Not for Luciano."

He regarded me thoughtfully and removed a pencil and notebook from his pocket and began to scribble. "My name is Batista. Fulgencio Batista. In five days come and see me at this place."

He tore off the page and handed it to me, got up, and left.

The rest goes down in history, as I say. When he became dictator, I had a friend at the top; we all had a tip-top friend. I used to be invited to eat suckling pig, which they called *"lechón,"* at his military headquarters in Camp Columbia, and we invested a lot of our good money together, and then came Castro, and it all went down the toilet.

When Batista left me that day, I had no idea he was going to go so far. But I decided I would look him up, as he had asked me to.

Chapter 14

While I was doing my business in Havana, Charlie, back in New York was embroiled with the more bloody business of Masseria and Maranzano.

Things were getting hotter and closer.

"They're knocking us bowlegged, Charlie. Masseria doesn't even come to the office anymore. Ever since they killed Mineo and Ferrigno, he's holed up at home."

Morello was worried. He'd aged a decade in the last six months, the creases around his eyes, the heavy jowls, were new to his once smooth olive-skinned face.

Charlie sat in his shirt sleeves in the corner easy chair of his living room, his hand massaging an ache somewhere near his scarred temple.

Morello continued, "Everything's going to hell in a red wagon." He studied Charlie, waiting for a reaction, some magic that would alter his bleak vision. "You listening to me?"

Charlie looked at him, his eyes cold.

"He won't see anybody but you. Maybe you can talk to him." Morello hated asking Charlie for anything. It made him feel his own discouragement and fear more keenly.

"All right," Charlie said flatly. "Let's go."

Masseria's house was a modest brick building smack in the center of Little Italy. The street smelled of sausages and onions and stewing tomatoes. Masseria's guards clustered on the front steps amidst the usual neighborhood goings-on. Boys played skelly with bottle caps, and old men sat in their undershirts playing checkers or dominoes. The street rang out with the voices of girls chanting jump-rope rhymes and their mothers calling down three and five stories to errant children or husbands.

In this atmosphere of normalcy Masseria's guards looked like freaks from another world. They chain-smoked and scrutinized passing cars with nervous suspicion.

Charlie found Masseria engaged in his favorite pastime: a vast platter of pasta sat before him on the dining room table, and his wife watched him shovel it in with all the fondness of a momma who relishes every bite her growing bambino consumes. When the older woman saw Charlie, however, her expression changed, and she rose, making excuses about the kitchen.

"Hey, Charlie, I hear your friend Lasker, he's in Cuba." Masseria appeared confident, ready to tell some of his favorite jokes. "I hear he goes into business for himself. He make enough money, maybe we take a bite out of *him*, too."

Spaghetti danced and jerked from his lips like dangling bodies riddled with bullets.

"You're taking too many bites out of everybody," Charlie told him blankly. "You're losing your troops, Joe."

"So I buy more," Masseria said with the petulance of a spoiled child. "Sit down," he said, nodding toward the chair his wife had vacated. "You want some dinner?"

"I'm not here because you're my uncle." Charlie sat down wearily. He was very tired of Masseria's games, his patience was limited. Practically vanished. "I joined up because I want Maranzano," he reminded the Boss.

"I got plenty of new shooters coming here from Sicily," the fat man told him as he broke off a wedge of garlic bread.

"That's what we need. Shooters from Sicily," Charlie said. "They can't find Grand Central Station, you tell them to shoot, they shoot the wrong guy. You're kidding yourself. They eat, but they don't win any wars."

191

Annoyed, Masseria raised his voice above a growl. "I hear a lot of complaining, Charlie. I don't hear any advice. Maybe you want me to lay down and die."

"That's what I want all right," Charlie shot back at him.

Masseria froze, his face tightened in a mean stare. He slammed down the forkful of pasta dangling in midair and splattered himself with sauce. Red splotches dotted his collar and cheeks like coagulated blood. He looked just like he'd been shot at close range.

Charlie softened, "Pull back and regroup, Joe. Pull our people off the streets. Don't give Maranzano any more targets."

"So then he keeps on coming on," Masseria said, wiping off his face.

Charlie said, "Let him come. Let him think he's won. Then nail it in; tell him you want to work out a surrender."

Masseria's eyes burned into Charlie's. He hated even the smell of surrender, like he hated the smell of burnt tomato paste.

"You're crazy! You're a lunatic!" he rasped like he was choking.

Charlie restrained him as he started to rise and call an end to the interview.

"When he thinks he's got it all his own way, we'll bring out every gun we got. We'll hit him inside his own house."

Masseria leaned back in his chair, studying Charlie for a few seconds; he scratched his hairy chest absently and then picked up his fork and resumed eating.

"Okay. I consider your advice, Charlie. I give it careful consideration."

Chapter 15

Charlie didn't seem to need me around in those days, but I found out years later how Ben was called back into the fold, when Charlie was feeling pretty desperate. Ben, of course, was flattered that Charlie chose to lean on him one more time. Benny had this thing about being needed—by Charlie, by me. I guess he had to prove he wasn't just another pretty face, if you know what I mean . . .

Ben told me that late one night the doorbell rang, he was walking his baby daughter, trying to get her to sleep. He had to put the squawling baby down, as Stella was out visiting with her mother's sister, Leah.

Taking a gun from his dressing gown pocket, he carefully opened the door a slit, leaving the chain lock hooked in place.

"Charlie!" Ben opened the door wide, pocketing his gun. His manner was cool. "I thought you forgot the address."

"I told you I'd call when I need you."

"When you need me? You picked some time of night."

Charlie followed Ben to the living room where Ben picked up his daughter and tried to comfort her again. "Hey, come on, gimme a break, sweetheart. What are you crying about? You already ate enough for a regiment. Shh. Come on."

Pacing the floor, Ben patted his daughter's back like he was carrying the Torah up to the bimah.

"I have to stop the war, Benny. We need a peace with Maranzano."

Benny crooned to his daughter, "You know about sleep? I'm going to tell you all about sleep."

To Charlie he said, "You going to kiss *his* hand, too?"

Charlie focused sharply on Ben's moving figure.

"I said we need a peace. When Maranzano thinks he's got victory, we'll settle up with him. For everything."

"What do you want from me? I don't even speak the language." His daughter was making quiet gurgling sounds now against his sopping wet collar.

"Somebody—an outsider—somebody has to pass the word." Charlie headed toward the bar and started to fix himself a drink.

"Make that two," Ben told Charlie.

Ben passed Charlie's message to Tommy Lucchese on a leafy bench in Central Park the next day.

It was safer meeting in the parks those days, for all of us. They had better police protection.

Charlie had inscribed for Three Finger a yellow monopoly card: "Go directly to jail. Do not pass Go. Do not collect $200."

This little marker was meant to serve as some sort of safe-conduct. Don't ask me why. It worked.

So Ben came along that hot July day near the Ramble with his coat hooked over his shoulder, licking an ice-cream cone: a hard one, as I recall: banana covered with chocolate sprinkles.

They met like long-lost acquaintances.

"How's it going, Tommy?"

"Benny boy, glad to see you."

"We're holding our own."

And so forth and so forth and blah blah blahbazoy.

And all the while Ben's licking away at his cone, sprinkles all over his lips. He said, "Holding your own is nowhere. Besides you're doing even better than that. I'm supposed to pass on this message: Charlie and Joe the Boss are sweet on each other and looking for a way out."

Lucchese took a white-on-white hanky from his pocket and stroked his brow with it. "What's that supposed to mean?"

"It means when Maranzano thinks he's got the world by the tail, he's going to get a bullet in his ear. The way you sit with Masseria, you're going to be dead about two minutes later."

Lucchese's hand froze as he moved to mop the sweat from his face.

"What exactly are you telling me, Ben?"

Ben had licked down to the cone, and was taking large crunchy bites from the striated cracker.

"The official message is, they want to work out a surrender. *That's* from Charlie. The rest of it, it's one of those guinea tricks. *That* you get from me."

Lucchese scrutinized Ben's face. "You'd do that to Charlie?"

"You did it to Masseria," Ben shot back, "didn't you? When your outfit's in the saddle, you owe me a couple of favors."

Lucchese watched Ben's passive face as he chewed on his cone contentedly. There was no hint of guilt, not a flinch. Tommy rose from the bench, took up his jacket with one hand and walked away from Ben, scratching his head.

Chapter 16

Headquarters for Cuba's banana republican army was Camp Columbia; this army camp, like any other army camp consisted of motor pools, barracks, a PX, a stockade, and a firing range. It also housed Sergeant Batista's rather palatial mansion and offices. Batista had been trained by U.S. Army cadres, could cadence count in English, and lived with Puerto Rican maids and Filipino scout orderlies on detached duty to the Cubans, as it were.

They say of that time that Cuba wiggled beneath the Dictator Machado's mailed fist. If so, the fist was also Batista's. As I was escorted to his offices, up past the aisles of oak and genip trees, flowering almond and flamboyant, each giving off a ripe scent like flowering honey, volleys of rifle shots rang out. I thought this was rifle practice, but later learned it was an execution.

Firing squads and flowering flamboyants. There's an old Nicaraguan folk poem one of the Somozas once told me, a long long time ago. "They are hearing shots near the cemetery wall. Nobody knows who . . ." And so on and so forth. The numerous armed sentinels everywhere seemed to have been placed between Batista and his republican army, like barricades of human flesh.

When I came into his office, heavy black fans were turning in the ceiling, and the guards snapped to so very smartly.

Batista wore the immaculate pressed suntan pinks of a Cuban army sergeant.

He rose to greet me. *"Compañero . . ."*

"Master Sergeant Batista," I replied. "Charmed, I'm sure."

Just then another volley shattered the silence.

Batista said, "I am strictly just sergeant first class here in Cuba. For a poor man, believe me, there is no higher rank."

"Claro!"

"Speak English," he said. "I am taking courses."

"Entonces," I said, "if a poor man gets to be sergeant first class, what's open to the rich here in Cuba?"

"Anything," he said, "a man could want or desire. General . . . colonel . . . minister . . . ambassador . . . But they are all just fools. Men of illusions. Vassals."

"Vassals?"

"Waste," he corrected himself. "Such waste, these illusionists. I have not seen their likes elsewhere, *ever*, I assure you. We sergeants run the army, Mr. Lasker. We learn how from you—excuse me—when you ran Cuba, and one day perhaps these same sergeants will run more than just the army."

He invited me to take a seat. "Either way," said Batista, "one way or the other. But let's get down to business."

"I have," he said, taking a deep tunic-stretching breath, in and out, at once, "prepared for you this certain document—under the authority of our butcher president, Machado. If anyone bothers you again, you will show them this. And perhaps, too, we should now be friends."

He handed me this new paper which looked just like a birth certificate: a parchment paper, with seals and stamps and deep embossing. "Take your fair share," said Batista. "Buy as you please, as much as you please. When you buy enough, all your friends will share in all your good fortune."

I remarked as that was how it probably should be.

Batista leaned back in his chair to scrutinize me, like a fly caught on his strictly official papers.

"In the sugar cane business," he said, "they have a saying, 'Ripeness is all.' The older the cane, the thicker and richer the crush of his juices. But as we also say down here, señor, *'con estes bueyes hay que arar.'* (With these oxen one must plow.) So I am saying. Enough. *Basta!* It suffices.

"I respect you, señor," he went on, "as a powerful man. Have you worked at very many jobs, Mr. Lasker?"

"Once I was a tool and die maker," I said. "Since then I've worked for myself."

"Me, I have cut the sugar cane," went Batista, "and plucked the wild genips from their branchy shawls. I was a railroad clerk, a railroad worker, a radio actor . . . even a barber. I am a very ambitious man. Someday I will be more than a sergeant. I will make my own power."

He leaned forward to select some papers from the neat stacks on his desk. "And now you will excuse me, Mr.

Michael Lasker." He was riffling through paper after paper. "There's a man who must be executed and I must make sure his certificate of condemnation is properly authorized and affixed."

He smiled, pure oleo margarine.

I asked, "What was this fellow's crime?"

"Displeasing me," he said. "Displeasing Machado. Displeasing Cuba."

In my final cable to Ruthie, sent via the Marconi Company on the day I was leaving, I said:

> Don't tell Walter Winchell but had lunch with some very ambitious young business persons today and we had an awful lot to talk about. My Spanish improving. The future of Cuba could be enormous. Should be cultivated. Real go-getting types down here, one in particular, a former army man. You'll meet him sometime. The salt of the earth. Hold the baby. I'm coming home. Stay sweet, Michael.

Chapter 17

Joe Masseria, the Boss, had gone along with Charlie's strategy. He took his men off the streets and let it be known he wanted peace. Joe, however, wasn't prepared to pay for his decision. And he was in a quiet rage the day of Morello's funeral.

"Morello, Charlie—let me tell you about Morello. He'd eat a burning coal for me." The Boss leaned mournfully against Charlie as they stood before the open casket. Morello lay in pink satin, a black silk suit and starched white shirt; his long manicured fingers folded over his chest, a star sapphire pinky ring sparkling, the only life emanating from his final resting place. Masseria stared at the waxen face of his loyal servant. "You know how many years, Charlie, how long we were together? They cut off my hand."

For one unnerving moment Charlie had a vision of Masseria's disembodied hand lying on top of Morello's pair in the casket. He blinked and shook himself back to reality, entwining his hand with Masseria's in an effort to comfort the mournful Boss.

"You still got a right hand, Joe. You got a strong hand."

Masseria closed his grip on Charlie's hand and patted it with the other.

"Morello was going to the meeting," he told the don. "The first meeting to make the peace. So they knew. They knew we were blowing smoke."

"Every gun, Charlie, every gun we got. I want 'em on the street."

An old man with watery eyes crossed himself at the casket and came toward Charlie and Masseria. The Boss embraced the old codger who whispered a few words in Masseria's ears, which seemed to renew his grief so that his large frame shook and big fat tears gathered on his jowls.

"Every gun," he repeated to Charlie.

"That'll come. Let them think we're hiding under the bed. There's something else first. Somebody betrayed us. Give me a few days to find him. I swear to God, I'll kill him with my own hands. Then we'll come out swinging with everything we got."

Again Masseria patted Charlie's hand. "Do it," he told his surviving friend.

Charlie turned to leave, and Masseria moved toward the casket to deliver a parting kiss to the stiff. A crucifix hung on the wall above the coffin. Hadn't Morello died for the sins of Joe Masseria? The old Boss brushed his lips against Morello's cheek. It was like kissing a highly waxed apple which smelled of perfume and formaldehyde.

Afterward Genovese took charge to make good on Charlie's promise to the Boss. He lost no time and met Albert Anastasia and Joe Adonis in Little Italy at the produce center, the day after the funeral.

"Everything I say now, I talk for Charlie Luck. Understand?" Genovese looked at these two like they were dead flowers not yet plucked from their stems, and they just nodded back, ready to follow orders.

"Come on. I'll buy you some fruit," Genovese told them. He took a large brown paper bag and strolled through the stands, carefully inspecting the best from the variety of fruits.

"Siegel was the go-between," he told them, fingering a bright yellow grapefruit. "He was the only one who knew—besides Charlie and Masseria."

Adonis picked up a particularly attractive cluster of green seedless grapes and twirled it by the stem, checking for rot and bruises.

"Look at that beauty," Albert commented on the grapes.

Genovese reached for them and dropped them delicately into a bag with a plop.

"We came out on the short end," Vito told them. "We all got plenty to lose." Then he addressed himself particularly to Anastasia, "The Brooklyn docks, they're going to belong to Maranzano, not Anastasia." He plunked the full bag in Anastasia's arms, and turned toward Adonis who began to fill another brown bag with figs.

"Adonis, you got your own piece of Manhattan. Kiss it good-bye."

"What do you want, Vito?" Adonis moved from the figs to tomatoes.

"It's what Charlie wants," he reminded him. "Charlie wants Bugsy Siegel."

"Then he'll have him," Adonis told him, "in a nice big bowl of fruit."

Anastasia laughed as the pair headed toward the cantaloupes, while Genovese was making his own exit around the sweet potatoes.

Later, reporting back to Charlie, Vito found him talking to two police officers.

"Sorry, Mr. Luciano." A sergeant was apologizing to Charlie for intruding. "Orders—questioning. You want us to wait for you downstairs?"

"Thanks. Be down shortly." The cops left and Vito looked at Charlie as if to speak. Charlie put a finger to his lips and said, "I'll call you later." Then he joined the sergeant who drove him to police headquarters and lead him down a corridor to Inspector Hearn's office.

"Shall I wait?" The sergeant was extremely solicitous.

"No thanks. I'll find my own way out."

Hearn was seated behind a large desk. His face was redder than Charlie remembered it when he disposed of the preliminaries.

"Now you listen to me, Charlie. We help each other out—big ways, little ways, we ain't waiting around for the Easter Bunny. You wanted to be picked up and brought in here so everybody knows where you are: that's *your* business. I'm not even going to ask what you got in mind. Now I want you to listen to *my* problem."

Hearn rose and moved around to face Charlie. He leaned his butt on top of his desk, standing above Charlie who was seated before him.

"Anything you say, Inspector." Charlie crossed his dangling legs; he hunched forward with his chin on his hand in a listening position.

"This Castellammarese War," Hearn continued. "You guys want to shoot up the rest of the country, the citizens out there don't buy my groceries. You start using the city of New York for a full-time shooting gallery, then we start getting complaints from the taxpayers. That hurts me in here," he tapped his heart. "Personalities aside, sooner or later somebody's going to ask me to make a lump on your head. So put a little ice on it, Charlie. Cool it down."

201

Charlie leaned back in his chair, tilting the front legs two inches from the floor.

"How do I do that?" he asked as if he were honestly expecting an answer.

"I haven't got a clue," Hearn responded. For him the interview was over. "Now if anybody wants to know, I brought you in here to ask if you got any idea who might've killed Pete Morello.

"The way I see it, Maranzano's bunch killed him," Charlie said automatically.

"Yup. That's a thought. Thank you very much."

Chapter 18

Ben Siegel came home one day from wheeling his new daughter in her pram and there were two fellows with guns pointed at him in his wife's bedroom: Adonis and Anastasia.

Stella was so terrified she couldn't utter a sound. The lead gun of Adonis was thrust hard into Ben's ribs. "Let's go, Bugsy," Adonis said.

I was still in Havana at the time packing to come back home when Charlie Lucky called with the news. It dampened my enthusiasm for the export-import business of molasses considerably. I thought, is this a sting? Or the games people happen to play? Or what—another murder? My friend Ben? Have a heart, will ya? There must be other ways.

I prayed a silent *kaddish* for Ben and went ahead to the sea wall in Havana to meet with Sergeant Fulgencio Batista one last time; I would be leaving for New York in the morning.

It was a tropical night full of stars and the incense of growing things. The dark sky had burst apart, brighter then all the lights of Havana, and the surf pounded at the shoreline like a bass drum. In a large luxurious bay windowed room on the Miramar, Batista in full uniform hardly seemed to work up a sweat over my news from home. He asked, "What do you wish from me, Michael Lasker?"

I thought we all might have to relocate pretty fast, depending on the political climates at home and in Cuba. "How much longer," I asked, "will Machado rule over this enchanted island?"

"Not long, I think," Batista said. "The isle is full of spirits of revolt. Revolt is in the air. You smell it?"

I smelled only the sea.

I asked what would happen after Machado's demise.

He shrugged, "We . . . the sergeants will have to rule Cuba," he declared, "for the better classes. . . ."

I proposed that perhaps we could each help the other.

He seemed to be waiting for this, for he said, "*Digame, señor!*" (Tell me.)

"Such a beautiful country as this," I said, "has a real big potential. Being so close to the States, plenty of Americans would be coming here to spend their money living it up."

"For the women?" he said.

"That too, of course," I grinned, "though I was thinking mostly of gambling casinos such as you don't have right now. The biggest and the best. Every game there is. No better markups anywhere. No better edge for us, too. The people just give us their money for a crack at luck. It's like they're throwing us bird seed," I added.

Smirking, Batista said, "I was thinking about all our Cuban children, Meester Lasker."

"We'd pay taxes," I hastened to point out, "just like any other legitimate business."

"*Who* are *we*?" he asked.

"You and me," I said. "Us."

203

Batista rose, and with one long finger touched the bridge of his nose. "When that damn butcher is gone, perhaps, and I am mixing up the *picadillo* here . . . *No?*"

"Yes," I said. "Of course. What will you need? *Guns? Money?*"

Framed against the glare of the lights rising out of Havana's steaming streets up toward the gay rosy auroras of the sky, Batista loomed very large, almost swollen by his own expectations of future power.

"We have guns," he whispered hoarsly. "*Basta! Basta! Bien campa.*"

"Go well, you too, my friend."

We shook hands, a deal of sorts: one hand laving the other. Batista said, "Until next time."

"*Patria libre,*" I declared: "A free country . . ."

"Or death," he whispered: "*Death,*" and then he slammed his hand down against his meaty thighs as if stamping out an executioner's verdict.

Chapter 19

The days were dwindling; Ben's abduction was on all our minds, especially Stella's, all the rage, you might say. Stella mourned him now as if he had been already found dead in a ditch somewhere.

Only Charlie seemed able to stick to business. How he managed, I'll never know. His own life was in danger, but he kept himself going, worked all the time, and sometimes in the evening he took refuge from the hurly-burly press of our murderous affairs at Abram Goodman's offices.

It had always been a pleasure to Charlie to see how Goodman had moved up in the world, his large new Manhattan office, the wall-to-wall carpeting and drape-enclosed windows, the big walnut desk looking out over the New York City skyline, big black Waterman pens, and cut flowers in silver bowls.

Coming in for a visit once, Charlie carried an unmarked bottle of clear liquor and placed it next to the brass paperweight in the shape of a fedora on Mr. Goodman's desk.

"Quite a view you got here," he told the aging hatter as he gazed out into the night at the lights of the Chrysler Building. "I can see my suite in the Waldorf Towers, too."

Mr. Goodman examined his gift bottle of liquor from the large black leather swivel chair behind his desk.

"Slivovitz, Charlie? Where do you find slivovitz?"

"You like it?"

"The only thing about the old country I like," he told him.

Charlie was pleased and turned from the window, smiling. "I got a case for you."

"No room. No room," grinned the hatter, within a hair of pouring himself a drink right away.

Charlie sat down on one of the easy chairs near Goodman's desk and politely declined the offer of a Havana cigar which his host offered him from a mother-of-pearl cigar box on his desk. Goodman lit his own, obviously enjoying himself.

"You told me once—" he began and paused, blowing the smooth smoke up into the air above Charlie's head— "I'm your oldest friend in America. You also had friends in Sicily?"

"It was a village—Lercara Friddi—they mined sulfur. That's all I remember—the yellow dust on my father's face when he came home from work. And the sulfur smell. A far cry from the odor of a Havana cigar, let me tell you."

Mr. Goodman poured himself a shot of slivovitz.

"And your old friends from the neighborhood? Mr. Ben Siegel?"

Charlie shook his head. "I don't know. We'll keep looking for him." He stared blankly past Goodman's glance.

"Where? They'll drag the river to find the right piece of cement?"

Charlie rose and felt in his pocket for a cigarette. He lit up a Lucky Strike and walked toward the window.

"Everybody dies of something," he said, his back turned to Goodman.

Abram Goodman swiveled around on his chair to face Charlie. "Sure. Something. I may be a hatter but I'm not mad, Charlie. You ever see Michael?"

"We have such different interests."

"Different interests—different friends," Mr. Goodman had that way of evaluating Charlie which always made him edgy, an almost maternal quality. Charlie picked up a new white rabbit felt hat, the token present that had always been a part of their exchanges.

"Thanks for the fedora," he said and walked before a mirror to adjust it on his head.

"*And you?* Do you ever see Charlie Luciano anymore?"

Charlie stared at his reflection, examining his scars. Goodman's timing had caught him off guard. He felt vulnerable and ignored Goodman's question.

"Joy sends her love. I'll send the slivovitz around." He turned away from the mirror, heading toward the door.

"Two graves, Charlie," said the hatter. "Two graves for revenge." As if these seer's words were haunting Charlie, he stood there very still, his back to Goodman.

"This war you're fighting with Maranzano. I sat in the hospital. I know what he did to you." Goodman did not care to relent: "Look at your *punim* . . . like a tractor has run over it."

Opposite Goodman, the skin on Charlie's face must have seemed taut and transparent in the lamplight, ghostly.

"Will you sleep so much better when he's in his grave?" asked the hatter. "When he's dead and gone, you'll have peace?"

"It wasn't Maranzano." Charlie's voice bore the promise

of death. "Joe Masseria did this to me."

The phantom of the opera; hearing Charlie's agonized whisper, Goodman almost choked on his slivovitz.

"Charlie. . . ." His throat constricted. Goodman always had a way of breaking into Charlie's vows of silence.

"That Sicilian brain of his," went Luciano. "Makes it look like Maranzano carved me up—to drive me right into his arms. That's where I went, Mr. Goodman. To Joe the Boss. That's where I am."

Goodman stared at Charlie, a mixture of confusion and pity on his face. Charlie would say no more. He turned and left the office, with Mr. Goodman calling, "Charlie, Charlie," after him.

The oldest friend of Charlie Luciano switched off the desk lamp. He sat for a while in the semidarkness, the slow burning glow of his cigar the only light in the room.

Chapter 20

I am not fond of travel, but I must say that the separations from Ruth that business has made necessary over our lifetimes have had their advantages. "Distance makes the heart grow fonder," and all that. Well, I think there's some truth to it.

The day I returned from Havana, Ruthie and I stood staring at each other for a moment before we embraced.

She stood at the head of the stairs, her long ebony hair flowing over a loose fuchsia robe, and I worshiped her from below on the landing, thinking I was the luckiest guy in the world.

"Michael?" She spoke my name with all the love a man hopes his wife could feel and started running down the stairs into my arms. I kissed her tenderly and held her away from me for a moment to devour with my eyes her face, her figure.

"Was it a good trip?"

I nodded. "A good trip." She hesitated a moment and asked, "Will it change things?"

"I think so, my darling," I reassured her. "Maybe a lot of things. I won't know for a while. Someday you'll see Havana maybe. I'll buy you palaces there."

"Michael," she spoke my name again in a dreamy way and took my hand, placing it against her stomach. Her face glowed with pleasure.

"I can feel him moving," she said then. She meant, of course, our child.

"How do you know it's a him?"

"You want a son—it's a him."

"Thank you," I told her, kissing her. She smelled of jasmine and mint.

On the morning Ruthie and I were basking pleasantly in our reunion, Charlie was taking his leave, though temporary, from Joy. It was a day of entrances and exits.

As Joy lay sleeping, Charlie dressed. He inspected himself in the mirror, and as on the day of his return from the hospital, touched the almost invisible scars on his face, like a blind man reading a map in relief.

Pocketing his wallet and keys that lay on the dresser top, he picked up the gun and considered it a moment before putting it inside the open drawer and leaving it behind.

Joy slept as he bent over her, kissing her tenderly. Even in her sleep she smiled at his expression of affection, and he stared at her face for a moment, as if to photograph her image in his mind's eye.

Charlie was headed toward Coney Island, and so was Joe Masseria.

Joe never said good-bye to his wife when he left his guarded compound in Little Italy. It was a superstition he and his wife had brought over on the boat from Sicily. If you say good-bye, you might never return. Instead Mrs. Masseria sat watching him from the dining room table. Dressed in black—like the old-fashioned Italian woman she was—black stockings, black shoes, Mrs. Masseria was always in mourning for one relative or another who had died from natural causes, or in some other way. She pretended to be mending a shirt of her husband's as she had done every morning for thirty-five years while he made his necessities prior to his departure.

Without exchanging a word, she held his jacket for him and walked toward the door, crossing herself the minute he shut it behind him.

Albert Anastasia got out of the black Packard as Masseria descended the steps and opened the door for the don, like a chauffeur. Adonis turned on the ignition as soon as Joe was safely ensconced in the back seat, and they headed downtown toward the Brooklyn Bridge.

Chapter 21

The Nuova Villa Tammaro restaurant in Coney Island was just off the beach, and a walk ran between the sand and the restaurant that looked out over the ocean.

Charlie and Masseria, flanked by Adonis and Anastasia, approached each other from opposite ends of the walkway.

"How long, Charlie?" Masseria faced Charlie head on.

"Three days. We'll talk. We'll get some lunch."

Masseria looked at the restaurant with interest. "Go on. Take a walk," he told Adonis and Anastasia. "What I need you for? Charlie takes care of me."

"We meet you here?" Anastasia was ready for the next order.

"I'll see you at the office." He waved his arms, dismissing them as he crossed over the walkway and entered the restaurant with Charlie.

Their table was laden with platters of pasta in red sauce, little squids in their own ink, veal piccata and veal parmagiano, lobster, roasted peppers, mussels in hot sauce and red wine.

Charlie and Masseria were almost the last diners, and a few of the other customers, over their tapioca puddings, stared incredulously at Masseria who sat consuming a feast they had assumed was intended for a large party.

"In three days," Charlie told Joe, "we'll throw a hundred guns at Maranzano's place."

Masseria gouged open the belly of a steamed lobster posillippo before him. "Everything goes bang, okay, Charlie?"

"You can have Maranzano for breakfast."

"I leave it to you," he told Charlie, mopping up some of the oily pepper sauce with his piece of Italian bread. "You serve me good, Charlie. I owe you plenty. You won't be sorry. I show you." Joe stuffed the sopping bread into his mouth.

"I'm the one that's grateful, Joe. You're giving me what I want."

"When Maranzano's dead," the Boss of Bosses told Charlie as he drained a large glass of wine and wiped his mouth with the back of his hand, "you carry it in your stomach—like good wine," he added patting his belly. "You've come a long way—from that time they arrested you."

"The day I thought you were in trouble with the police?" Charlie inquired, sipping slowly from his demitasse cup of espresso.

While the waiter cleared the table, Masseria leaned forward and patted Charlie's hand. "We both put our troubles away."

Masseria pushed a large plate of pastries aside and brushed some crumbs away with his napkin.

"Come on. You work too hard," he told Charlie as he cut a deck of cards he had in his pocket and prepared them for a fast shuffle and a game of pinochle.

Again Charlie was presented with the cards for cutting, but he shook his head at them, doubtfully. "I got a lot to do . . ."

"An hour, a little sixty minutes," said Masseria with feeling. "It ain't going to kill you. Come on."

He stuffed his mouth with a piece of cannoli and started to deal. But Charlie stopped him and cut and dealt the cards himself.

"A good meal . . . a game of cards," went Masseria. "Charlie, what else do we work for? You think I want to be the richest man in the whole country? Relax, Charlie Luck. . . ."

Charlie put some money on the pile of bills on the table and told Masseria to do the same, but as he picked up his hand, the glass of red wine nearest his cuff overturned and some of it spattered Charlie's Palm Beach suit.

"Nice going, Joe."

He pulled back from the table, picked up a napkin, dipped it in some water, and rubbed at the wine stains.

"What's the difference?" Masseria said. "Forget it . . . come on, Charlie, I'll buy you a new suit."

Charlie rubbed and rubbed and then he got up and headed for the bathroom. "Be back in a minute."

He was going to try a little soap on his stains.

Masseria called out, "I'll introduce you to my tailor, Mr. Miller in the Rockefeller Center."

Masseria in an unguarded moment, picked up Charlie's hand and peered at it a moment, and then his own.

In the bathroom Charlie was washing his hands again and again under cold water, letting the wrists freeze up under the rush of the cold.

As Masseria glanced up from Charlie's cards, he saw Bugsy Siegel enter the restaurant just as alive as Charlie and I had planned him to be. He was also quite well armed.

Next to enter were Vito Genovese and Albert Anastasia and Joe Adonis.

All armed.

All executioners.

Masseria leaped to his feet; his hand went out for the weapon in his coat pocket, but he was cut down before he could shoot back, by heavy fusillades of pistol and machine-gun fire.

And still Charlie washed his hands, and still Masseria's riddled body pulsed with the impact of more bullet wounds.

A pin cushion . . . a regular pin cushion. I swear.

Genovese told me his last words were Italian: *"E io che non ho fatto mai male a nessuno!"* (Literally, "I who have never done any evil," though it also could mean "never hurt anyone.")

Now Masseria was so much mountainous oozing dead flesh. A whole empire of crime crushed and buried under by bullets, like Pompeii or whatever, and a surprised, still look on his bloody face as he met those he might have guessed would get him one day.

In the days that followed our myrmidons killed many more, too. Charlie's torturers from the warehouse were cut down by Lepke's and Gurrah's slugs. Even the guy who had been on that dark street pleading for a handout on the night of Charlie's abduction was cut down with one swipe of a barber's razor as he sat waiting to be shaved.

We were enthroning a new Dynasty of Crime by getting rid of the old.

That all began with the murder of Joe the Boss Masseria on April 15, 1931.

Coming out of the washroom that day, Charlie saw his body sprawled among plates of food, and masses of gouted flesh and blood. In his dead hand was the ace of diamonds.

Charlie notified the police himself from a telephone in the restaurant. He said he personally didn't have any idea how it happened. He'd been in the washroom.

Afterward he sauntered out of the restaurant as crowds began to gather and crossed the boardwalk toward the beach below where I stood.

"Finito," he told me with a grin and savage pride. "It's done. A long life's worth . . . for me . . . for you, Michael . . . and for Abram Goodman, too."

Sirens were wailing nearby.

I said, *"Aumein,* Charlie. *Amen Selah Hallelujah."*

The death of Masseria signified the restoration of our old friendship and association. Charlie, Ben, and me were united now as never before. In fact the forces of Salvatore Maranzano would soon learn that it had never really been broken.

Just how long our friendship would survive depended on all the battles still to come. But this I will leave for a second volume of my memoirs.

The bottom line and final prize of the struggles that ensued would be the absolute control of the national crime syndicate, or Corporation, as we prefer to call it.

Now as I look back over all those years from my vantage point of a silly dying and vain old man, every bit as much a criminal and self-deceiver as the best of them, I think all we have for ourselves is courage, and luck, and money, and of course, the gift of life and what we make of it.